Bolinas

Thomas M. Barron

Garbage Wagon LLC
San Francisco, CA

Bolinas

Copyright © 2019 THOMAS M. BARRON

Cover art by David Powell
Creative Director Toby Petersen
Editor Jennifer Lewis
Polish Editor Courtney Pazin

Published by
GARBAGE WAGON LLC
San Francisco, CA

Library of Congress Control Number: 2019903457
ISBN (print): 978-0-9997033-3-5
ISBN (ebook): 978-0-9997033-5-9

Printed in the United States of America
1   3   5   7   9   10   8   6   4   2

For those that are close
but feel so far away.

1

"Look how nice it fits you!"

"Mom, uhhh, shoulder patches? That's not really my vibe."

"But you look so handsome! And you have a real job now!"

"It's the same job I've had for over a year." I scratch a phantom
itch at the collar. I write mediocre love advice, via social media. My
mom pretends that I'll be teaching at Amherst in the fall.

We're both talking but not to each other—more near each other.
Because neither of us is fully listening. There are only two of us in the
room, yet we each have our own agendas. Plus, the Christmas tree
looks too perfect. It makes me sad. There's something depressing
about something without flaws. It might be the jetlag. I was in Australia
yesterday.

We criticize our mothers because we are close. We spite them,
because we think they don't know us. But that is untrue. They just

know us in a different way. Maybe that's what love is. To not fully pay attention but to always show up.

She opens her gift.

"So beautiful! Thank you!"

"That was my favorite place to swim."

"It's in Sydney?"

"Bondi. One of Sydney's eastern suburbs. Next door to where I stayed in Bronte. If you don't want it, I'll take it."

"Of course I want it!"

"Trade you for a sportscoat? May need a bit of tailoring."

"George! You're terrible."

"I know. I love you, mom."

"I love you too, sweetheart."

It's late on Christmas afternoon. There aren't many gifts under the tree. My mom, knowing me better than I know myself, takes the small one she had for Shawna and makes it disappear.

Shawna.

Fuck.

We need to scroll back a little more.

•

Shawna told me she was pregnant a week ago. She claims it was mine. Fidelity is not really her jam, but I went with it. Fortunately, I was having sex with my dead best friend's sister at the time, to optimize the guilt. Was it the best decision I've ever made? Nope. But if you'd met her, you'd understand. She was a queen. She is a queen. Suzanne. And she didn't judge when her brother, Craigo, and I killed a guy. The guy was a pedophile, a woman beater and was planning to adopt PJ's baby. PJ was my best friend. My best friend on earth. An abusive stepdad scenario was not happening.

•

Pasadena, CA

Photo: Christmas decorations on a drought-proof front yard.

@georgeous If Santa's sleigh reminds you of a baby stroller, you're probably walking into the house of your ex-girlfriend. @plan_b

"HI!!!"

"Hey."

"Oh my god you're here! Look!" She thrusts mistletoe over my head. I recoil but catch myself in the door jam.

I give Shawna a chaste kiss and look over her shoulder at her mother.

"Merry Christmas, Ms. B."

"George! So nice to see you! Thank you for coming!"

"This is for you. Sorry, if I had more time, I would have looked for the sommelier at LAX."

"That's so lovely, thank you! And you know me. I drink wine from a box. Anything with an actual cork is a real treat."

"That, I know." We share a smirk.

She pulls me in for another hug. It's a hug that says you and my daughter have been through a lot. You haven't done the best job. But you haven't done the worst. And you're a bizarre part of our family. Oh, and I'm pretty confident that this is the last place on earth you want to be right now.

•

Shawna's mom leaves us to go work on dinner, which I'm confident is already ready, awaiting my arrival in the oven. Shawna and her mom are tight. Super tight. Surely her mom knows that her pregnancy terminated. And all Shawna wants is a little time with me alone. Based on her hands not having left my body since I arrived, I'm thinking Shawna wishes we had a clean twenty minutes.

Maybe twenty-five.

•

Even though I'm ten seconds from being thirty, I've had quite a few firsts in the last ten days:

1. First time I've ever been an accessory to a murder.
2. First legit pregnancy scare.
3. First time I've had health insurance in two years.
4. First time I actually don't want to have sex with Shawna, since the moment we met.
5. Re: #4—correction: since the first moment I saw her.
6. I swear.

•

"How's your mom?"

"Good. She wasn't even passive aggressive about me being gone for a year."

"That probably made you feel worse." She gives me tender eyes and sees an opening. Slides her hand onto my knee.

"It did." Shawna knows me even better than my mom. That's why

I've never been able to shake her. "How are you? About not being a mom?"

From smile to frown, in under a second.

"Really? Great segue George. Jesus fucking Christ."

"Heeey. I've been worried about you. I just wanted to know that you're OK. I'm sorry. I could've waited a few more minutes."

The hand she removed from my knee returns.

"George. I feel off. We've been so distant. And then I had part of you in me. Literally, growing inside of me." She pauses. I can't help but glance at her stomach. "And even though I was super freaked out, I was, I dunno, happy. Excited. It's true. Even if it sounds a little stalkery."

"Just a little."

"George."

"No, it doesn't. I totally get it. I swear."

"But I also feel relieved. Super relieved. And I'm sure you do, too."

"You know, I feel kinda similarly. I'll be honest; I was relieved. But there's still some sense of loss. I dunno. I can't put my finger on it."

•

"Are you sure you don't want to stay? You know my mom doesn't care."

"Yeah. It sounds weird, but after being gone so long, I'm excited to sleep in my old bed."

"Do you want me to come?" She giggles, hopeful. She knows she can break me. She's done it a million times before.

"Shawna. You've been through a lot. I know that. Do I want to make you happy? Yes. Am I attracted to you? Yes. Do I want to hit the reset button and go through all of this again? No. I really don't."

"George, no one is asking you to. I just miss you. And now you're home. Panama and then Australia? It's like I've been waiting for you for fourteen months." This is false. Her Instagram betrays her. But I leave it. "And now you're here. You're actually here. And you're gonna go sleep two miles away?"

I have no idea what to say.

"It's tempting."

"Don't overanalyze it." She pauses. Seeing if she needs to bring the hammer. She does. "George, we were gonna be going to the abortion clinic this week. Together. Or talking about co-parenting. And now all of the relief I felt from not being pregnant is being replaced by anxiety that you don't want to have anything to do with me. And I think it's because you felt trapped. And now you don't. I feel like you're gonna jump on this opportunity and disappear again. Even if all of that is true, please please please don't just drive away from here. Not tonight."

Please please please let my mom's old Accord start on the first try.

•

"Shawna. I've been idling for five minutes."

"Then turn the car off."

She removes her hands from the doorsill and crosses them. Not as a defensive posture. Because she's cold.

"Can I please go home?"

"Unfuckingbelievable. I'm fucking throwing myself at you, and you're choosing a car with ripped seats over me. Fuck you, George."

"I love you. I do. But I cannot restart this. I'm sorry. I just can't do it. It makes me too sad."

"So that's it? You're just ejecting? Completely? From us? You're done?"

I take a few deep breaths. Hoping one of them comes out with words. The harshest two word sentence in the English language.

"I'm done."

Tears well up in her eyes. I've already let a few slide down my own cheeks.

She walks away. I glance at her in the rearview, about five feet past the bumper. She turns back. Then stops at the bumper. Shakes her head.

Frustrated, she grabs the antenna with both hands. Trying to break it. It's a 90's Honda, but it's still a Honda. She can't break it. All she can do is bend it, like a cowlick from a bad haircut.

She bends it.

She shakes her head in disappointment. Not at me (I don't think). At herself. For letting herself throw this tantrum.

She speedwalks back to her mom's house.

Shawna has been in this car a hundred times. She knows that the radio has always been broken.

•

From: Rogers, Timothy

To: Lewis, George

Subject: Training, Money & Life Skills

George—

Welcome home. Even though I won't see you for ages, it's still nice to have you back on domestic soil.

I am a little busy forecasting next year's advertising revenue, so forgive me for being all business. As your direct manager (which still seems a bit ridiculous), I do need these things from you:

Annual Training:

If you don't complete this on time, you'll have to wait three months to become a full-time employee with benefits. You'd be surprised at how often this occurs. I'll have Lydia coordinate with you taking it in the San Francisco office.

Money:

The move from freelance contributor to Staff Writer is a substantial bump. Yes, taxes will happen. But Esquire's retirement package is more than competitive. And a recurring legitimate salary may change your life for the better. Please make all of the necessary automatic deposit/retirement fund selections in the package Lydia emailed you. Welcome to adulthood ;)

Life Skills:

Doing your homework paid off. Your Tweet queue is complete until April. I know you tend to tweak/modify them constantly, but please don't. Legal has already approved them, and the magazine is looking to synchronize digital and print content.

Therefore…insert drumroll…your dream of pursuing a Life Skills piece has come true.

In addition to your Novice Learns to Surf concept, the Head of Features wanted to know if you'd consider taking karate? It sounds odd, but we're doing a big pictorial to celebrate Bruce Lee's birthday, with a bio, etc. A Novice Learns to Karate Chop series may offer a nice balance. Lydia has already contacted a dojo(?) in downtown San Francisco and pre-authorized payment for five classes. You are welcome to decline, but I suspect you won't. For your over-curious mind, this is right up your alley. HiYa!

Please keep in mind that even preapproved articles only have about a 10% chance (at best) of making it into the magazine. It's the way of publishing. But don't let that impede the quality of your work.

Merry Christmas, and let's connect live in the New Year.
Best,
TR
PS If you haven't yet, you might want to consider starting a blog. Something personal, where you develop your own brand. Esquire may not be around forever, and you'd be smart to have your own following.

Never, ever, tell a writer that he has met all of his deadlines and can…

Disappear.

•

My mom has given up on me. Another reason why I love her. Because my mom is still here.

"You can't just go to Hermosa? Surfing was invented here! I'll never understand why you must always go so far away. You're so peripatetic." My mom knows fancy words, like *peripatetic*, because she teaches at Pasadena Community College.

"I will come back, I promise."

She responds with the face of disbelief.

It's not unfounded.

•

It's a '99 Dodge 1500. Sure, I wanted a classic Westfalia. But this thing could tow a VW. And it won't need to be towed. Pragmatism outweighs novelty. $7k with power windows overrides $30k without. But damn, every time I look at the roof, I wish it had a pop-top.

•

"I love you, George."

"I love you too, mom."

She's already crying, and I'm pretty close. I really, really need to come home more.

"Do you even know where you're going? You have maps?"

"Mom. I have my phone." But I open the glove box and show her the paper maps I got from AAA. "Couldn't help myself. No battery required."

"That makes me feel so much better. Be safe!"

"I will. See you soon."

History suggests that these are both lies.

2

When you least suspect it, you see it. Out of the corner of yet another sweeping turn—the ocean unfolds. It lays across the horizon sleepily, like an over-washed comforter.

I'm an hour outside of LA, but it feels like a world away.

I can't believe I own a car. A van. A bedroom on wheels. A loud bed on wheels. Damn the engine is deafening. But I couldn't be happier to be rambling along in this second-hand old man's dream ride. Always buy your cars from a single owner, with all of the records in a crisp, tidy file. Ideally? An old guy who doesn't really want to let it go as much as his wife does.

And I'm not alone in my van romance. I pull off in Ventura. About twenty others have the same idea. Van, truck, van, car, van.

The Fairgrounds. Both a location and a proper noun. Every surf spot has a name that's more of a narrative. Two words and every local will know where the spot is and under what conditions it works best. Say Rincon or Hammonds to any surfer that's ever driven between Ventura and Santa Barbara, and watch their eyes light up.

Instant calm hits, as I drink in the ocean view and kill the motor. But the engine's aggression is absorbed and repurposed by the derelict next to me.

•

The Beach Boys made Ventura famous as *Surf City*. But that was the 60s. Now? Due to disparity, it splits the chasm between rich city and meth city. I don't know what it is about the ocean that draws people without purpose. Therefore, there are a ton of burnouts, a handful of wine bars and, like everywhere else on earth, honest people just trying to get by.

I pull into a spot.

The guy parked next to me looks a little too longingly at my board. I pull it out and gently set it wax-side down on the grass.

"Wow. She's a beauty. Balsa?"

"Yeah. Solid. A gift. I'm just learning. Not sure if I picked the right spot. Don't want to get my tires slashed." I gesture at the van. "I just dropped seven large on this bad boy."

Here's the goal of my statement:

1. Surfers are territorial.
2. I'm parked right next to a fully equipped Carrera. Mentioning the price of my modest Dodge can't hurt.
3. You've gotta be respectful, if you want any intel from locals. Especially surfers.

4.   Never drive a nice car to a surf spot.

"I think you'll be OK. Just wear a leash. And head way down. To the south part of the beach. It's easier to get out anyway. Your car's good. Can't say the same for the one that's parked right next to you."

He fondles his car keys and eyes the Porsche's pristine paint job.

Ventura, CA—The Fairgrounds

Photo: Locals-only sunburnt surfer, next to his '85 Ford pickup, Porsche in the background. Both Porsche and burnout's teeth are shades of yellow.

@georgeous Don't know which attitude to express while in a foreign land? Especially a new surf spot? Go with deference.

·

PJ and his brother, Craigo, taught me everything I know about surfing: most surfers are assholes, I'll be one of them pretty soon (fortunately, I'm already an asshole), surf spots are secrets and *Guitar Center's* tagline—*We only sell one thing: the greatest feeling on earth*—was surely stolen from surfing—it's that good.

·

I suit up and paddle out. The balsa floats like a dream. It's 11am on a Tuesday, and there are dozens of people out. Welcome to California.

I catch one and fall.

People hate falling. But in surfing, it's inevitable. And I love it. Out of the thousands of miles I've swam in pools, jumping in has always been my favorite moment. Being underwater, completely submersed—it's divine. That's why I don't mind crashing into the ocean.

The board tumbles through the white wash, yanking my leg as soon as the leash gets taut—hyperextending my hamstring. Ouch. Reminder: bend knees more. That's probably good advice for all the time, not just when surfing.

I catch another.

Ride the line for three seconds. It feels like a month.

I paddle back out into the lineup. One guy nods, having seen my ride. I smile.

Another guy with something to prove accidentally (?) flicks water at my face, as he paddles by.

Local dickheads. How original.

And that's why I'm headed north.

To Bolinas.

•

Bolinas is an hour past San Francisco, but it may as well be on the moon. It's an unincorporated pocket of a town with no police force, great white shark infested waters and just one bar.

It's the perfect spot for this sojourn. Close enough to an *Esquire* office but far enough from LA. A place that's somewhere but also nowhere.

It's the exact place I want to be.

And I'll be there tonight.

I pull over in Summerland.

It's the first time I've parallel parked the van, since owning it for two days. It drives like a monster marshmallow. When I get a spot right in front? It's the first time the van feels like it's really mine. An extension of me. Even more so, since the fish sandwich I'm about to get from Tinkers Burgers will probably leak tartar sauce all over the front seat.

The van would be so useful for moving things. A couch. A mattress. A dead body.

·

I've been to San Francisco a few times. But not like this. You drive up the coast through rolling hills. The air gets a bit sharper. The tension builds as you wind through Silicon Valley, past SFO with its enormous tarmacs.

Then you crest a hill on 101 North.

And.

And.

Bam.

The whole city explodes.

You want to pause, for just a moment, and take it in. Fortunately, you've got all the moments you want. Because you're stuck in soul-crushing traffic.

Still, it's a pretty cool view.

·

Nothing is more motivating than a new job. With a publishing company that's been around for a hundred years? You don't want to screw it up.

So, TR's ask of me—to take five karate classes—I take as a direct order.

Bruce Lee created his own martial arts discipline. He was practicing mixed martial arts decades before the UFC and reality TV.

Bruce Lee's style is called Jeet Kune Do. Translation: *Intercept the fist*. The movements are small, efficient. It teaches practical violence as a response to unavoidable aggression.

Jeet Kune Do combines boxing with fencing and kung fu. TR's broad use of Karate was not on point. But being on point is not his job. It's mine.

•

Be Like Water Marital Arts is a one-man shop. A second floor studio in a decaying glass mini-mall. It's one of those relics built by someone trained to build in the burbs—unaware that the turns, steps and alcoves that add dimension to a suburban strip mall don't work in a city. Instead, the added nooks create infrastructure for homeless encampments. And places for drug deals. And mugging tourists. It also sits at the bottom of a steep San Francisco hill, collecting trash. I'm surprised this is the place *Esquire* picked. But I like it. It's a gritty place. A place where work gets done.

Getting trained one-on-one doing something so intimate, I had to do a drive by. Idling in the van across the street, I appreciate the simplicity and lack of pretention.

Class is in session.

Like a creeper, I watch. A dad, who looks like he should be selling rental insurance, instructs a young, manicured professional. You'd think it would be the other way around, since Dojo Dad is wearing track pants and a t-shirt he probably paints in. But his agility, his grace—he's swift. Lethal.

No intense branding or tiger murals. Just a guy teaching another guy how to defend himself, in a small room made of too much glass and not enough Windex.

Even voyeuristically, I'm pretty sure this skill is gonna come in handy.

●

The van is happy to no longer be navigating the narrow hills of San Francisco. And so am I.

So far, this has only been a road trip. But as soon as I cross the Golden Gate Bridge, I know I'm close. I'm gonna get to write a real story, learn to really surf and connect with my long-lost best friend. Watching the big winter swells roll underneath the bridge at dusk, I can see them through PJ's eyes. See them like a surfer.

●

After getting gas and getting lost, I don't make it to downtown Bolinas until well after dark. The road fatigue hits. It hits hard. I park in front of Smiley's, the only bar in town. It's unnervingly quiet. The thought of trying to rustle up some fun sounds too tiring. I read for a bit and am dozing before I turn off the battery-powered lantern.

It falls.

Dink.

The lantern is magnetic and likes to sleep on its own pillow, made of metal.

●

A restless night.

The only sleep involves a nightmare.

A warzone at sea. Scanning for my ship. Alone.

My sleep has become so wrought with torment, I welcome being woken up. Even if the greeting is less than cordial.

Knock, knock, knock, knock, knock.

"Sir, you can't sleep here. This isn't a campsite."

I'm pretty sure I'm not the first person to sleep in front of Smiley's, nor will I be the last. I shake it off, but damn the van bed is comfortable.

Do they actually teach cops a certain kind of knock? Or is it the fact that they always knock with a piece of equipment, instead of their hand, that makes the sound both unsettling and sobering? Regardless, it delivers the exact behavior they seek: compliance.

"Oh! Hey! I'm sorry! So sorry. I drove from LA last night. Just wanted to get the lay of the land. Got here and…"

"Understood. Glad you were safe. Just don't make a habit out of it. OK?"

"Yes sir."

•

A coffee. A bagel. A hurry-free drive through the surrounding coastline. The wind is blowing pretty hard, and I find myself back in my exact same parking spot in front of Smiley's.

Bored. Restless.

Solution? A beer before noon.

"Hi!"

If a bookishly attractive female lights up when she sees you? And she's a stranger? It's not because you're handsome or charming. It's because she's in the service industry. Never mistake professionalism for flirtation. Picking up bartenders and servers is ungracious.

"Hey."

"Getchya somethin'?"

"On the fence. Was gonna go surfing, but it looks a little blown out."

"Yeah, the wind's been on it for a few hours. My roommate said that south will hit overnight. Tomorrow morning might be good."

"Good to know. Craving something light. How's the Fort Point Kölsch?"

"The KSA? It's the yummiest."

"Sold."

She flips her laptop around toward me.

"Here, you can check Surfline, if you want. But the WiFi is suuuper slow."

I type three letters, and Surfline is already in the browser history.

"Awesome. Thanks."

"Where are you from?"

"That obvious, eh?"

"You're too tan. Look at your neck, and look at my neck."

She's right. My whole body is a golden swimmer's brown.

In a few more years, if I'm not more diligent about sun protection, I'll look like Kurt Vonnegut's last days before I'm forty. Not said pejoratively. Vonnegut was the king.

She catches me daydreaming. I'm the only one saddled up to the bar at Smiley's. She can easily reel me back in.

"See?"

She yanks her shirt down to show her wetsuit tan line. The rest of her is lighter—the color of chocolate milk. And her muscles look like they came from work. Real work. Not spin classes.

In one deft movement, she slides a coaster across the bar, drops the KSA, leans toward me and pulls the elastic at my neck.

I've had such a weirdly traumatic last year; I don't even flinch at her move. And my calmness surprises her. She drops her hand, letting the elastic of my neck snap back into place. It leaves a small sag, where her finger was.

"Sorry!"

"No, no. It's cool. I've never been called out for being too tan before. I'm much more of a swimmer than a surfer. And where I learned to surf, it's lack of a tan that makes you stand out."

"Really, where?"

"A few times in Panama. But I didn't really stand up until I was in Sydney a few weeks ago. Got the bug. My name's George. From LA. Sorta."

"George? Such an old school name, for such a young guy."

"After my uncle. I turn thirty next month, so not so young." I extend a hand. She grabs it. More delicately than I expected.

"Maya."

"Great name. After Maya Angelou?" It's a total guess, because she looks ethnically ambiguous. Jet black hair. Big chai-colored eyes.

"I dunno? But that would be super-duper cool if it was, huh? And I'm twenty-eight. Not far behind you."

"That would be an intense namesake. A lot to live up to. But there's probably something poet-worthy about pulling beers in a north coast beach town."

She examines my beer: 80% gone.

She pulls another and sets it in front of mine. Superb service.

Nope.

She picks it up and taps my glass in a one-person cheers, then takes a sip.

"Welcome to Bolinas."

·

Bolinas, CA—Smiley's Schooner Saloon, est. 1851
Photo: Smiley's exterior, including decades of weather damage.
@georgeous If you want to do the most obvious thing in the world: crush on a bartender. It's not gonna end well. @smileyssaloon

·

Bolinas is a weird place. I recognize that anywhere I go is a weird place. But this place is super weird. It has a weight to it. It's foggy like everywhere else around here. But that's just part of it. Somehow the fog in Bolinas is thicker, denser. The redwood trees are beautiful, but they add to the severity, the seriousness. It's a heavy place.

·

I walk out of Smiley's, stuffing the address Maya gave me in my pocket. It's a small farm, where I can park the van and crash for a few days. The place where she stays. It may not be her actual phone number, but it's close.

I stuff the slip of paper into my jeans and pull out the van keys.

Some guy is leaning against the van. I hit *Unlock*, and he doesn't even blink. He saunters his gaze toward me. His buddy is staring straight into the van, with his cupped hands acting as shade binoculars on the glass.

I clench my teeth, awaiting the inevitable townie confrontation.

"Road warrior! Poppin' in for a brew? Not safe to drink and drive."

"Yeah, I was thirsty. Long drive. How'd you know?"

He's tall. Looks at me eye to eye. And wiry. He's got those veiny muscles that guys get from pulling the wings off of flies.

"Bugs. On your windshield. Parking sticker says Glendora. You from SoCal?"

"I'm George." I throw out a handshake, not backing down.

"Johnny." He takes my hand and overtakes it, asserting his dominance.

Prick.

He stares me down. His immaculate Carhartt jeans suggest that he's some sort of pseudo trustafarian. That he doesn't really wear work clothes for work.

He pulls his Bolinas Border Patrol t-shirt off his shoulder. Showing more sinewy muscle.

"And that is?" I nod to his sidekick, with the wispy pot-smoker's mustache.

"Liam."

"Liam, the doors are open. You can quit smudging my windows and go inside." Liam looks at Johnny for approval. *Can I? Can I go inside?*

Johnny pauses for a moment. Off-put by my openness. So am I, to be honest. He stops leaning on my van, almost deferentially.

"SoCal Surfer? We've never seen y'all bring a balsa board to Bolinas."

Y'all? Really?

"Observant. That entire board is covered up by the board bag."

"Yeah, but look." Johnny looks over his shoulder at Liam. Liam entered through the sliding door and has already yanked on the zipper of the board bag. "The tail is sticking out. It's got glassed-in skegs. Either an old board or a throwback. Where'd you get it?"

"Sydney. Australia. It was my best friend's."

"He didn't want it?"

"He's dead. Murdered." And if he was here? He'd knock your teeth out.

"Oh. Sorry, bro." He snaps his head back to Liam. "Liam! Come on. Get out of the guy's van." Frazzled, Liam scrambles out.

"Dude, sorry!"

Liam tries to wipe his handprints off my windows, only to further smear them.

"Nah, it's cool. Bought it from an old timer. Kept it cherry. Using it as home base. Trying to learn to surf. As a way to honor my friend."

Johnny's moment of compassion is fleeting. He slides his hand across the hood of the van, like he's grazing the lower back of my girlfriend. Familiar.

It irks me.

"Bolinas Border Patrol? Is that your band?" It's weak. But it's all I can think of.

"Hah. Nah." He looks down at his chest. Not un-admiringly. "Bolinas isn't incorporated. We're the volunteer…uh…cavalry." He corrects himself. "We're caretakers. Makin' sure all is well in our little hamlet." Other than the word *hamlet*, he's dropped into a forced drawl that is half Alabama, half *Deliverance* and mostly hostile.

"Really? I talked to a Bolinas cop this morning."

"Marin County. Sheriff, not a cop." He gives a knowing smile to Liam. Liam returns the smirk, obsequiously. "They only drive through once a week."

"Lucky me."

"Liam. Let's go."

Liam complies. He pulls away from my van reluctantly, as if he might want to date it. Who could blame him? Johnny bro-wraps an arm around his shoulder. He turns back to me but addresses Liam.

"Let's take the edge off a hard day's work." It's 1:30pm. "See my girlie, girl. Maya." He exaggerates his fictitious drawl. "See yah 'round, SoCal Professor."

"Stay outta trouble, Johnny."

Opening the door to my van, I glance across the passenger seat. It's a redlined piece I was working on for *Esquire*. Looks like a graded term paper. Hence him calling me *professor*.

I don't hate it.

•

My phone buzzes. Mom.

"Mamacita, what's up?"

"Did you make it?"

"Easy peasy. Compared to last year? A few hundred miles of freeway? With access to gas and snacks every thirty miles? I love America."

"Oh, good. I hate the idea of you driving so far alone."

Her comment makes me wonder if the drive will end up being the least dangerous part of this trip.

Probably.

•

After chatting with my mom for ten minutes, I wake from the cell phone haze and realize that I've walked all the way down to the beach. It's sunny. And gorgeous. Just a tinge colder than the coldest day in LA. Yet, there's still something unsettling about it. It's too beautiful to feel completely safe.

Wups. I left the van unlocked.

"Hey mom, I've gotta run. I forgot to lock the van, back downtown. That is, the five storefronts that make up the downtown."

"Oh dear! You should go! Bye!"

Unfortunately, I've already absorbed the Bolinas cadence. My walk back to the van is sleepy, even though the LA in me is concerned.

About four car lengths away, I see what must be Johnny's ride—a lifted four-door Toyota Tacoma. The dead giveaway is the 2 Mile Surf Shop sticker. Bolinas locals are infamous for removing the *Bolinas 2 Miles* road sign, to keep non-locals from being able to find Bolinas. But that makes people want to find it even more. Including me.

Wait.

What?

A striking female sits in the backseat of Johnny's truck. Long, straight, light hair and fair skin. Baltic-looking. Very young but with a severity about her. Exhaling cigarette smoke. She's got the window down. Her smoking is awkward, forced. Like attempting a job you're not qualified for. Or, more likely, don't want in the first place.

Bolinas, CA—Bolinas People's Store
Photo: Restless female smoking in back seat of Toyota Tacoma.
@georgeous Waiting rooms aren't only in hospitals.

I put the van in reverse and look over my shoulder, catching another glimpse of her. Unnerving.

Hmmm. Johnny, King of the Bros, has an impatient female in his backseat. Yet he opts to go into a bar to flirt with Maya? Odd. Really odd.

Turning onto Sir Francis Drake Boulevard, I pull behind an aged art car, covered in painted glued-on seashells. Bolinas traffic. It gives me a chance to look back at her.

Something about her vacant stare is haunting.

3

The farm is a little outside of town. It's the spot Maya wrote down on the piece of paper. Where I can crash for a few nights, without getting hassled. A small operation, specializing in earth-friendly veggies. They're a dime a dozen here in Bolinas.

•

I've got some time before dark, so I drive the thirty seconds to the other side of town—to buy beer and do some scouting. The liquor store is adjacent to a used bookstore. My kind of place. And the latter may not exist in another decade.

I'm drawn to a *Maritime Law* spine. It's a dusty tome and weighs more than my arm.

"What an oxymoron!" The friendliest man of Indian-descent engages me.

"Huh?"

"*Maritime law*! What is that book? A thousand pages? And it only needed to be one page! Total! Because the only law in maritime law is no law!"

I'm confused. Plus, he's wearing a scarf draped like a pashmina. Too chic for this driftwood town.

"I've heard it's pretty vague. Hard to enforce. Do you work here?"

"No one works here! Look!"

They have a self-pay policy: *Ordinary Books $2, Extraordinary Books $4, Pretty Great Books $5…*

"That's insane. I know I'm not supposed to advertise this, but I'm from Southern California. That level of faith in humanity is completely absent."

"Ha! It's not faith, it's fear! Vigilante policing by a bunch of outlaws and ruffians! The only difference is they have boats instead of horses! Est-ce pas terrible!" Is using *ruffians* and a French accent conversationally permitted outside of an Elizabethan Faire? Only if you're a man wearing Hermès.

I drop a ten in the cashbox, which I'm convinced has a camera on it. *Maritime Law* will make a great bedside table for the van. He gives me a big grin, as I turn to exit.

"I'm George."

"Raj."

"Both one syllable names. A rarity."

"Isn't that charming!"

•

The smartest thing I packed in the van? A hundred-foot long

extension cord. Because my camping spot at the farm? It's eighty feet from the house.

Don't worry. I left a note, a bottle of cab and a six pack of Fort Point on the porch, as it seems to be the local favorite.

If you've never tasted Bay Area water, it's delicious. Even the hose I'm lapping from has a hint of Britta, as I rinse out my wetsuit.

How do you think Northern California surfers spend most of their time?

a) Scouting swell

b) Surfing bombs

c) Looking cool

d) None of the above

It's d. An hour surf session requires a diligent, and I mean diligent, wetsuit drying ritual.

In addition to my laptop and phone, I need the extension cord for the fan I brought, if I want the suit and my booties to have any hope of drying. My wetsuit is a bit funky from sitting in a plastic tub for a day and a half, after getting in the water in Ventura. Hence the re-rinse.

It seems a little self-serving to rinse out my wetsuit on the porch of my hosts, but they're way ahead of me. Two Patagonia women's suits hang, drying on a fence next to the hose. A big bottle of Dr. Bronner's old school peppermint soap is also in play and presumed communal.

•

Now that *Esquire* pays for my beautiful, beautiful iPhone and the service contract, I can tether my laptop to my phone to send a few emails. But the data overages must cost a fortune.

From: Lewis, George

To: Rogers, Timothy

Subject: Re: Training, Money & Life Skills

Tim—

I made it! So far, I love this assignment. Get paid to learn to surf and write about it? It's criminal.

A few housekeeping items:

1) Bolinas as a site location is working out great. It's the perfect spot to demystify this sport.

2) Healthcare check. Direct deposit check. Retirement contribution check. It's confirmed—I am now an adult.

3) Lydia forwarded my cards to the San Francisco office. That will really make it official. Is it OK to wear flip-flops to the posh 44 Montgomery Street address? Kidding. I will be there for training, dressed appropriately. I promise.

4) Surfing: I know you asked me to forward these directly to the creative team, but you have known my voice for such a long time, I hope you don't mind me bouncing the initial drafts off of you. As you said, it's episodic. These don't have the same urgency as the Tweets. I hope that's OK. A rough draft of Surfing #1 below. Emphasis on rough.

5) Same as above—will keep you posted as I progress on the karate

class front.

6) For Esquire's magazine piece on Bruce Lee, might I suggest this quote? It's been around the block, but it's still really good, "Be like water making its way through cracks. Do not be assertive, but adjust to the object, and you shall find a way around or through it. If nothing within you stays rigid, outward things will disclose themselves."

7) In full transparency—the quote above is lifted directly from the Be Like Water Marital Arts website. Thank you again for the opportunity to work on that piece.

8) Blog suggestion: that's good advice. I've been doing the poor man's version by capturing a few moments on Instagram. Sometimes I write them and don't even publish them. But I wouldn't say no to one more follower...@georgeous

Surfing #1

Ralph Waldo Emerson said it best: We are forever preparing to live, yet never living. The same goes for surfing.

Waiting for swell. Driving. Looking. Finding. Committing. Suiting up. Paddling out.

Actually riding waves? That's just a moment.

Then how do you practice? Focus on agility? Cutbacks? Getting to your feet quickly?

Nope.

Practice paddling.

It's the most critical part.

Paddling gets you out.

And paddling gets you in.

Paddling catches the wave for you.

The rest? Either you can learn it or you can't. But paddling is the ticket. Because paddling is hard.

Best,
George

George Lewis
Staff Writer

•

Knock, knock, knock, knock.
"He's not quite ready."
"Huh?"
"Your landlord says get up!" A raspier voice. Still a female. But not Maya. I pop my head up.

I open the van's side door. I'm glassy-eyed, in my underwear. Both of them are in wetsuits, pulled down to their waists, with bikini tops on. The waft of air chills my nipples, and I'm not alone.

"Dawn patrol. You ready?"

"Dawn patrol? He looks more like yawn patrol."

"I can be ready in two minutes."

Maya opens the door of the van, dropping my wetsuit on the carpet. Her friend chucks a steaming towel at me.

"It's warm? Amazing. Thank you. I'm George."

"You're welcome. Francesca. But everyone calls me Frankie."

Of course they do. Maya rubs her fingers on my wetsuit and frowns.

"Warm towel, but your suit is only half dry. Yuck."

I do a crouched deck-change. The towel is as welcoming as the wetsuit is not. Having two women watch me drag on a wet wetsuit? It reminds me of trying to type with someone looking over your shoulder. Self-conscious. And my towel could be bigger.

•

My patrons bound ahead. Maya picks a wildflower and smells it, while I put on my booties. They're both barefoot, but I don't care. I'm freezing.

"Thanks for waking me up, and thanks so much for letting me crash. You two are so nice."

"Ha!"

"I know, right?"

An inside joke. At my expense.

"I'm serious. I'm really appreciative. I hope that doesn't sound sarcastic?"

"We know. We're teasing. We always joke about importing guys into Bolinas. Surely you have witnessed the man-talent around here?"

"I have."

"A guy that brings wine and only sneaks glances at our tits on the sly? And with clear guilt? That's a win. Stay as long as you want."

•

It's cold. And early. They paddle out effortlessly. I'm close behind, stroking as fast as I can.

"Damn it's cold. Does it ever warm up?"

"Yeah, in the summer. You should come then."

"I spent the last five seasons in the summer. I welcome the winter." They look at me, puzzled. But I take a deep breath of foggy air and savor the taste—like taking a drag off an open freezer.

"That was a joke. The summer is exactly the same in Bobo. But it's worse. Because of the wind."

I look across the various breaks.

"Do you guys want me to go down there? Stay out of your way? The likelihood that I fall is one hundred percent."

"Everyone has to learn sometime. Plus the locals will be up shortly, and you may want to stick by us. They're not super welcoming."

"I know."

"You do?"

"Like Johnny and Liam?"

Maya pipes up.

"You know Johnny?!"

"Maya's taste in men. Well it's…" Frankie gives me a playful yet discerning once-over.

"Huh? You and Johnny?"

A wave comes. Frankie takes it. I paddle over the top, barely escaping the lip. I'd kill to be able to see a wave, turn, paddle twice and catch it. Someday.

My eyes return to Maya. We've got two minutes alone. And she can see that I'm committed to my question.

"You seriously dated Johnny?"

"This is a small town. Really small. And, as you witnessed, I do drink at work."

"Who doesn't?" She can tell that I'm not being flippant and smiles. But the smile disappears.

"When I first got here, I was…"

"Lonely?"

"Yeah, sorta."

"You're not a local?"

"Nope."

"From where?"

"Phoenix."

"Ooof. The only place on earth worse than LA."

"Yeah. It was killing me. I needed to come here."

"I totally get it."

We both watch the horizon for a moment. Small waves roll in. But nothing big. Nothing that requires action.

"Why do you care? And how do you know him, anyway?"

"He was scoping out my van. The moment I left you at Smiley's.

He was waiting for me."

"Ahh. Right. He's a bit territorial of Bolinas."

"He's your boyfriend?"

"No!"

"But…"

We both watch Frankie approach. She got a nice long ride. Her eyes get big, and she yells at me.

"Go go go!"

A set wave is coming straight at me. She's telling me to paddle. I do.

I catch it.

But this wave is a little bigger than what I'm used to. Shoulder high. Powerful. I get up on my knees, first. Mistake.

I wobble up, lacking confidence.

But as soon as I stabilize, the wave lines up. A straight shot. The balsa digs in, knowing what to do. I shift my feet the teeniest bit, to stay in it. It reminds me of Craigo, dancing along the board like a lusty Latin dancer. Intimate. Subtle. Responsive. Everything that I am not. I miss that guy.

Then it's over.

The shock of the water reminds me of the original owner of the balsa. PJ. A moment of sadness.

But I am quickly reminded to do exactly what PJ would want— have fun, at all times, at all costs. Hence attempting this damn fickle sport.

Bolinas, CA—Pacific Ocean
Photo: A chilly, perfect right-hander opening up above the nose of the balsa.
@georgeous Even adults need playgrounds.

I try to kick out of the wave gracefully, like a 50's surfer with short shorts and perfect hair. Fail. Instead, I almost knock my teeth out and bruise my shoulder on the edge of the board. The balsa? No damage.

Reaching up to grab the rail of the board, my eyes catch the path that leads to the parking lot.

Team Brolinas.

•

Bolinas has a few breaks. They're spread out. But on a clear day, like today, you can see all of them. We're at The Patch. Johnny and crew? They're heading to The Groin. The expert's spot. Every town on earth has its allotment of alpha males.

And maybe I'm becoming one of them.

4

Sleepily pulling out of my makeshift campsite, even the van can feel the apathetic weight of Bolinas. I can't believe you can drive here in a day from LA. It feels like another planet.

Edging into the empty old town, one person is up. Raj. He sees me. We share a smile. He's watering a makeshift street garden. Green onions? The thought of pouring water on anything in this town is absurd. You could sweep a glass across the foggy air in front of your face and it would come back half full. Or half empty.

Planting in an overrun community garden. Such a thankless job.

Bolinas, CA—Pacific Ocean
Photo: Raj, dominating his world and not afraid of whitening strips.
@georgeous White teeth. Green onions. @crest

•

Imposter syndrome. It's a real thing. Titans of industries suffer from it. And so do I.

Today I have a big boy day. Training at *Esquire's* San Francisco office. Then research at Be Like Water, where I need to embrace my inner aggressor and remember as much of it as I can for the piece. Turning my hands into deadly weapons? It'll be a slight shift from doing it with a pen and a keyboard.

•

"That's a lot of stamps."

"Not really. All of those trips to Costa Rica or even Colombia were just to keep my visa from expiring. It's easier than trying to cross the Golden Gate Bridge at rush hour." It's the truth. And a very mediocre joke. Mediocre jokes are the currency of friendliness.

"Bay Bridge. People commute on the Bay Bridge. The Golden Gate is just so nannies and Whole Foods delivery trucks can get to Marin." The *Esquire* office manager is eating up my charm. "And Australia?"

"Yeah, that's…"

"I'm kidding, cowboy. Twenty stamps at twenty-nine? It's good, but Hunter S. Thompson you're not."

"True."

For some reason, I had pictured an aloof supermodel at the front desk. Not a bridge and tunnel sudoku addict. San Francisco is not New York.

•

"All done. Do I meet with the attorney, now?"

"Go back to the kiosk. I'll call Suzanne over."

A familiar name. My last bedmate's name. Just hearing it said aloud, a fondness washes over me. And I miss her snark.

"Complete?"

"Yeah. I didn't picture sexual harassment and ethics training in the same format as online traffic school. I thought you taught the course?"

"In person? We used to. But it got too expensive. Now? Everything's in the cloud."

She looks over the printout of my answers.

"One wrong. You pass. Sign here."

I sign and glance at my mistake:

True/False: Derogatory humor is never acceptable in the workplace, with the exception of light-humored jokes that are self-effacing.

How could that not be true?

•

Business cards. The first ones of my life. They're sitting on the dash of the van. Next to the $64 receipt I paid to park. Maybe San Francisco is a little like New York.

I thought the indoctrination into corporate America would be more…ceremonial? It's anticlimactic, like everything else in life.

The first recipient of my new identity? The van. I jam three business cards into the broken defroster vent that rattles constantly. Perfect fit.

•

Bruce Lee #1

"Sensei?"

"Sifu."

"Oh, right. Sorry. I'm George." Sensei is Japanese for teacher/master. Sifu is Chinese.

"The writer."

"Yeah, sorta."

Possibly the most intimidating guy in the world. He's so serious. He doesn't over-enunciate when he asks a question.

He looks me over in half a second. I try to keep my gaze open, real. Honest.

"Why? Why are you studying?" Not combative. He, too, extends honesty.

"Well, Esquire…"

"No." He taps his finger on my chest. On my heart. "Why do you? Why do you want to study? We all have assignments. But we each take them for different reasons. It's rarely pure obedience."

Good question.

•

Immersion journalism means writing about something you've experienced directly. But it can still be a lie, because I often write what I expect something to be like, first, before doing it. The unpolluted version is always helpful. Always. And more often than not? It's dead on. Except in this case. It's dead wrong. What an understatement.

"Hey there!"

"Nice to meet you, Sifu. I'm George."

"Nah, just call me Mark!"

Without hesitation, he unbuttons a floral shirt that's two sizes too big. Then off come a pair of tattered khakis, a size too small. Swapping them for his same paint-stained t-shirt and track pants from the other day, I don't think my hour session will impede him from booking a flight to Fashion Week.

He sets a thick dad's wallet next to a first generation iPhone. Then he turns, excited.

"OK! Let's see whatchya got!

•

So, so sore.

Even turning the key in the van hurts my shoulder.

Looking back at the dojo, eh, kwoon, it's hard to forget what he said.

"This may seem backwards kiddo, but the first lesson is how to kill someone. Pretty crazy, right?" His eyes pop wide, like he's softening the blow of a chemistry pop quiz.

"Why?"

"Because it's way easier to kill someone than to just hurt them. Isn't that bananas?!"

Such a sweetheart. Although, for his birthday, I might get him an eyebrow trimmer.

•

I don't condone day drinking; I champion it.

If there's a juicy parking spot in front of a place that looks interesting in San Francisco? Snag it, before it's gone.

"You see dee street parking sign?" The owner of the restaurant points. "It's the 7am. Early one. The street parking on the Polk Street. Is early. For overnight."

"Uhhh, it's only 2pm. I think I'm good." Does he really think I'm gonna sleep at a parking meter?

"OK. Good. You like dolma? You must try. Come."

•

By 8pm, I'm drunk, feeling the odd spunk that follows seven pilsners and four small plates of rice wrapped in tea leaves. *Dunya*. A little Mediterranean place that is nearly invisible when you pass by. But as soon as you walk in? It feels like your local spot.

Kandur is Turkish. Speaks four languages. Parents were refugees. All he cares about? My love life. My new best friend.

"Dis one. With the child. You are done, eh?"

"Yeah. I think so."

"Do you wan to have baybah with her?"

"No."

"OK. Is done. We have the progress."

"I guess."

He sighs.

"You wan to move back to Australia? Be with dis wan? You wan her as your lady?"

"Jesus."

"So no."

"Uhhh…"

"In Turkey, we say, 'He who has never been burnt by the sun will never know the value of shadow.'"

"OK?"

"When you wan the shadow. Does she gives you dis?"

"When I am sunburnt, do I seek her for shade?"

"Ugh. Americans. Always dee literal. Yes or no?"

"Yes or no what?"

"Man cannot live without shadow. Eh shade. Can you live without dis wan? If you can, den she is not dee wan."

•

6:55am. The street cleaning behemoth around the corner wakes me, saving me a $500 ticket and a tow. I don't think Kandur charged me for the last three beers. But I'm paying for them now.

•

A beautiful, windy drive up the Bay Area coastline.

Until I hit the second of the only two stop signs in Bolinas.

Johnny.

He's lazing around the side of the road, half on the shoulder, half on the pavement. Is this a fucking roadblock?

"Do you ever work?"

I'm feeling cavalier, having blocked fifty slow-motion punches yesterday.

"Could say the same 'bout you, Professor."

"That's not true." I want to toss him one of my coveted business cards. But being prideful solves nothing.

"Jes came from an important business meetin'?"

"Why do you care?"

He grits his teeth. It backs me off. He's got nothing to lose. It's intimidating. And he looks like he'd actually enjoy hurting me. A sentiment we both share. "And I did just come from work. But I'm more of a cog in the machine than a boss. So no, not important."

"Everyone's got their role. Glad you understand yours."

Johnny could teach a class in bullying.

Fuck him.

"Where's your girlfriend?"

He takes a breath to say something but doesn't. I realize he's not sure who I'm talking about.

"Where's yours?"

"I'm not stepping, man. Was just impressed by your game. The blonde female? In the backseat of your truck? Kinda Baltic-looking?"

"Ohhh, yeeeah."

"She's gorgeous. Where'd you guys meet?" How does it feel, motherfucker?

Johnny does not dig the tables being turned. But I do.

"We're friends. Helping her out a bit." He gives a mean smile. It says—*no more questions.* "Need to get backaddit. You be good now, professor." His unsubstantiated drawl is back. We all have our crutches.

•

Maya and Frankie are tackling one of the endless tasks involved in running a farm. Fix this. Move that. Weed. Weed again.

They are roughly the same size, but the difference in their movements is stark. Maya acts as more of a helper. Everything she does is small and graceful. A finesse player.

Frankie is much more competent and much more forceful. Her boat creates a big wake. But, if broken, she could probably fix the boat.

"Want help?"

"Always."

•

With only one bathroom, I take the last shower. Brief but still hot. Since my other towel is still wet, all I've got is my backpacker's towel.

"On the sink!" Maya sneaks a hand through a sliver of the door, setting a fluffy towel on it. "It's clean. Dinner in a bit!"

"You guys are always bringing me towels."

"But you're gonna need to dry yourself."

•

Frankie is marinating the salmon filets I brought back from the city. Three overturned milk crates act as a makeshift outdoor island next to the barbeque. Maya is back in the house, lotioning in her room. I smelled it, when I walked past.

I'm holding both of our beers. Frankie grabs a different one every time. I don't correct her.

"You've got sunscreen on your cheek, still. You surfed? It's flat."

I wipe both checks.

"I swam."

"Where?"

"To Stinson."

"And back?"

"And back."

"Really?"

"Yep."

"Holy fuck. You said you were a swimmer. But that's legit. How long did it take? Two hours?"

"A little less. But I got out and bought a Kit Kat at that little market there."

"That one that smells like rotisserie chicken?"

"Exactly."

She hands me back her (my) beer and looks at me, with a question that is more of an invitation.

"Do you wanna stay here? Until you're done?"

"The whole time?"

"How long? A month?"

"Maybe two more weeks."

"You do need somewhere to stay, right?"

"I do. But, I saw an open studio and a granny flat, since it's off season. You two have been amazing. But I'm not a charity case."

"You've brought food or booze every day. And you're not afraid to get dirty." She grabs my right hand and turns it over. "Although it's clear you don't do it often." She rubs a coarse thumb against my soft keyboard hands.

"I'm not rugged?"

"You don't even have those callouses the gym guys get from doing pull ups."

"Caught."

"BEERS?" Maya yells from the house.

"YES!" Frankie yells back. I involuntarily step back, from her yelling next to my ear. "Oh, don't be a baby."

"Fair." I take my last sip. "You know, this is a fake place."

"Two loud bitches that feed you and bring you drinks?"

"Not that exact word choice, but…"

"That exact sentiment."

"Not untrue."

"George. Hang out. We can use the help. And the entertainment. Seriously. And Jesus, you're sleeping in your van. It's not exactly The Four Seasons."

Maya rolls out with our drinks and drops them.

"Here you go! Gonna grab my juice box!" I believe this refers to her coveted box of rosé in the fridge. She turns back toward the house.

Frankie's eyes follow her. Then she turns them to me, with a serious look.

"But staying here means staying in your van. OK? I know you and Maya have a little thing going on, but just don't. OK?"

"I wasn't planning on it."

"It hadn't even crossed your mind?"

"I'm on a break from decimating women's lives. Especially when I'm a tourist."

"Good. And what about me? Did that even cross your mind, for a second?" She sets down the barbeque tongs and quickly covers her eyes with her hand. "Do you even know what color my eyes are?"

"They're hazel. Like mine. And we both have auburn hair and freckles. Not the most original combo. Although your freckles look sun-kissed and mine look sun-damaged. But I will not answer your initial question, because…because I don't want to. Also, how many KSAs have you had?"

"Four?" She smiles. I see five dead soldiers next to her, and she's halfway through number six.

Bolinas, CA

Photo: Frankie in her element, looking charming, with her mischievous grin.
@georgeous Barbeques should have drink holders. But then I'd be out of a job.
@frankiethetankie

We cheers.

"Maya has a little crush on you. I can tell. She's also addicted to being desired. So just don't, OK? Johnny destroyed her. And she doesn't need to be destroyed by both a nice guy and a criminal."

"Unfortunately, I don't know the difference."

•

We have a magical night.

I, for once, don't drink too much.

They stumble to bed, talking to each other loudly.

I zip up my hoodie, for the crisp walk to the van.

•

From: Lewis, George

To: Rogers, Timothy

Subject: Be like water

Tim—

1. Training complete.
2. Forms complete.
3. My employee # is 06723 (yes, I find this exciting).
4. Business cards in hand. Such expensive cardstock for the digital age. Classy.
5. Bruce Lee 1 of 5 complete.

I'm warming to the life of a semi-corporate citizen. Especially as I witness *Esquire's* matching contribution to my 401(k). I am now $481 closer to retiring!

My only struggle is with the Bruce Lee vignettes. I took my first class. It was awesome. And intense. I wrote three pages of notes. Do you have any guidance? Any guardrails I should consider for the piece?

The Sifu (Chinese for Sensei) is cool. Not what you'd expect.
Thanks again for such an amazing assignment.
George
P.S. Rough draft of second surfing installment below.

Surfing #2

Armor. The Spartans wore it. The few brave enough to serve in our controversial foreign wars wear it. And us weekend warriors create our own versions of it—Lycra, sunglasses, special shoes and face paint also known as sunblock.

A wetsuit is the same. It even feels like chainmail, with its snug fit, endless zippers and Velcro. Once on, it impedes your movement. But it also makes you a bit fearless.

Fearless to paddle out into something that covers three quarters of the earth's surface. A force that makes and breaks continents.

We suit up in $500 neoprene, grab a fiberglass sword and fight a fictitious battle. We duel with the ocean for a few seconds. The glimpse of conquest, before an inevitable fall.

•

A true waterman rises and sets with the sun. –Anonymous.

Too true.

You know you live on a farm, when it's 5:50am and you wake up fully rested. Because you went to bed at 8:55pm. Frankie calls 9pm: *Farm Midnight.* Genius.

I didn't surf yesterday, and my wetsuit is fully dry. The small luxuries. Rambling through the fog, I'm oddly excited to go surfing alone.

5

Wet and cold from the water, I see a ticket on the van. Nope, a note. I grab the corner of it, with my wet fingers.

G—Favor? When Maya wakes up, take her to the city? The delivery is late, and we need two new kegs by tonight. We're hoping you can grab them in the van? If you can't, don't worry, we'll figure something out.
Frankie
P.S. Solo dawn patrol? Impressed.

•

7:30am.

I rinse out my wetsuit and do a drive-by Maya's room.

Door wide open. Face down. One of the farm cats is laying across her neck, like an airplane pillow. I guess I'll go downtown for coffee.

•

To say Bolinas is fixed in time is an understatement. One of the studios I found for rent was posted on the bulletin board at the Bolinas People's Store. Yes, handwritten on a 3x5 card. Widespread internet use is still another decade away.

Coffee? You've got to order it from the host stand at Coast Cafe, the only spot that serves breakfast.

Small, small town.

•

Coffees in hand, I walk back to the van. Carrying two drinks always brings me back to feeling like I have a girlfriend. Or at least someone of interest. It reminds me of Suzanne. And the pact I made with myself to not get involved in anything for a bit. To stop breaking hearts and maybe heal my own.

The screen door slams shut behind me. A common sound to anyone within a hundred feet of the store. But it catches my attention. A young woman walks toward a beat up Ford Ranger, holding a box of tampons. Another attractive Eastern Bloc female in Bolinas? And guess who's driving?

Liam.

Her arm sways back with the box, as she reaches for the pickup's door with the other. It's a slight movement, but it pulls at her shirtsleeves and exposes both of her wrists. Both have one thing in common—a thin red line of severe irritation. Wrists that have been bound, maybe with twine but probably by zip ties.

•

Barely awake, Maya looks like a bird nested in her hair. Her puffy eyes come across 10% sleepy, 90% comfy. She wears it well.

"Do you know where you're going?"

"I can get us to San Francisco. Surely you know how to get to the brewery?"

"That's a lot of faith"

"Do I have a choice?"

"Um, you have a phone. But yeah, I know where it is. In the Presidio. So pretty."

Her finger directs. Highway 1 to 101, cross the Golden Gate Bridge, enter the Presidio. Find a place to park.

On the way, Maya asks if we can pull over and take a picture.

San Francisco, CA—Golden Gate Bridge

Photo: Two heavily bitten fingernails, but still painted, crushing one of the bridge towers in between them.

@georgeous Wouldn't we love to live a life of only beginnings? When the smallest gestures enchant us. @holdthemayannaise @sephora

"How are your articles coming?"

"Good. Slow. But that's OK. There'll be so many rounds of revisions, a month to develop a draft is nothing."

"Sounds nice. Super flowy."

"Are you kidding? It's maddening. Take however long you want, but if you take too long, your content will be obsolete."

"Just hearing that gives me anxiety. Is that what it's really like?"

"Absolutely."

"Huh. From the outside, it looks fun. Like a dream job."

"It is. Sorta. But you also feel like you should always be working. So, even though there's a lot of downtime, it's hard to turn off and enjoy it. Idle hands are devil's tools."

"A devil, you're not. Why does every good boy want to be a bad boy?"

"I dunno. It's funny. You calling me out for being a good boy. You're hardly a lawless renegade yourself."

"Oh really?"

"Look." I grab her hand, gently. This move reminds me of her grabbing my t-shirt at Smiley's. "You work on a ranch. Organic, sure, but it's legit. It's real work. And you bartend. In a tough bar."

"A farm. I work on a farm. A ranch is for livestock."

"Ugh. That's not my point. You paint your nails. And not pink or candy apple red, a sophisticated color."

"It's only to keep me from biting them. Can you guess the color?"

"Uhhh. Guy's version? Brown. Actual guess? Cappuccino Cinnamon Swirl. Still, it ain't pink. The earthiness of it says that you know a few things but don't need to advertise it."

She looks at her nails and then sets them on the radio dial.

"It's Fallen Leaf. We're close, but let's listen to some music, while we have reception?"

•

"Carlos?"

"That's me. How can I help?"

"Hi! I'm Maya! We spoke on the phone? This is George."

"Ohhh, right. The delivery fail. We're so sorry. That truck is still in the shop. But let's get you fixed up. Are you parked out front?"

Two dudes wheel out the kegs. We end up getting four, because we can. It's unclear why everyone does not drive a van. So functional.

Carlos hands over the invoice. He gives a nod to one of his guys, who returns with a few six packs of beer. Um, mine?

"We took 20% off. And of course waived the delivery fee. The canned beer is just to say thank you for the business. The IPA is our best seller, but the KSA is my personal favorite."

"Mine too. I love the slightly lower alcohol content. You can just sip one all day."

"We're pretty committed to functional alcoholism."

"Aren't we all."

Maya teeters on her feet, waiting for an opening in our bromance.

"My business partner…" It's a funny way to describe Frankie, because she's so much more. "…said twenty percent, plus our next two deliveries would be free?"

Her voice stammers. I can tell that this wasn't her idea. That Frankie wanted to grind them a little bit. The ask is fair. But it's polarizing for Maya—the antipode of her pleasery ways.

"Oh, yeah. Yeah. I saw that on the notes. But I'll doubly confirm when I get back." It might be a lie, but his delivery is solid. Affable.

And two people, acting awkwardly as others' proxies, survive another day.

•

It feels nice. The silence. A forty-five minute drive back, and we don't even bother listening to music. I don't know anyone else that could tolerate this, let alone enjoy it. But it's also all of the turns that pull you in. Give you something to look at. Interrupt your thoughts. If we were on a straight freeway for over an hour? The presence of my passenger would make me fidget. And I'd squirm right into some estrogen-fueled-power Top 40. My choice, not hers. Beyoncé can salvage anything.

Peaceful meandering turns or not, I'd kill to know what she's thinking.

Let it come to you. Advice I have given before but rarely taken myself. I want to ask her a million questions. But I hold off. Letting her choose when to engage. The patience pays off.

"Do you ever think about staying?"

"Where?"

"Anywhere."

"Of course."

"But you've been to such cool places. It seems like it's hard for you to sit still."

"Yeah, I could see how you'd see it that way. I actually crave an obstacle. Even a bump in the road. Something that would promote inertia. Impede my movement. I just haven't yet. Even though I seek it. Growing roots sounds fantastic. To be totally honest? I'm tired."

She marinates on it.

"Is that really true? Or do you just say that? Until you find it. And then find a flaw with it? It's like romance. Do you really like the girl? Or do you just want her to like you?"

•

"You got four! Oh, I'm so happy!" When you get to please someone who is difficult to please? Very satisfying. "You just saved us a fortune. This week at Smiley's? You drink for free." In an unexpected display of warmth, Frankie gives me a side hug and kisses me on the cheek.

During our hug, her hands fall naturally at my waist. Then she squeezes my hips, intimately.

After we mount the first keg and wrestle it into the fridge, Maya and I roll the other three into Smiley's ancient walk-in. The fridge is forty degrees, but I'm dripping with sweat.

"What does a keg weigh? Two hundred? Jesus you two are strong. All that farm work."

"I can't believe I used to pay money to workout. We call living here the 'Barn Method'." Maya flexes her bicep.

"Brilliant."

"Close your eyes."

"OK?"

She reaches up and pulls my head down. Maya's short; she's either telegraphing an MMA head butt or a make out. She kisses me. First on the mouth. Then on each cheek. It's slow. And sweet. A moment of surrender. She releases my head.

"That was a one-time thing."

"A pity kiss?"

"Stop it. You know I like you." She strokes my arm. Throwing me a bone but also letting me down. "You've been so nice to us. And you keep to yourself, which is my favorite thing about you. Not pushy."

"False. I basically moved in with you guys within two days of meeting you."

"All the other guys that come over follow us around like puppy dogs, until we fuck them or fight them off."

"Jesus."

"Seriously. George...thank you."

A charity kiss? It pushes my buttons.

It should be a perfect moment. But I can't enjoy it. It's too manufactured. Like the GMO Christmas tree at my mom's.

"Maya. I'm curious about you. You're fascinating. But that? Don't do that. If you want to thank me? Buy me a beer. Don't kiss me and then take it away."

•

"The kegs stayed pretty cold on your drive. And now, for once, we have two spare. Shall we sample the merch?" Frankie, even though she is the queen of tough love, is an incredible diffuser. She senses our tension, the minute we walk out into the bar.

Her question was rhetorical.

•

Do we get wasted at Smiley's?

Yes.

Do we walk home cold, hugging, listening to the waves crash and the wonderful silence of the fog, like romantic idiots?

Yes.

Does Frankie peel off, leaving us alone, because maybe she's given up on keeping us apart?

Yes.

Does Maya, turn to me, tell me how cold it is and ask if I can keep her warm?

Nope.

•

7am.

There's no colder sleep than sleeping alone, when you were teased all night that you wouldn't. Eight KSAs foster way, way too much hope.

I'm not in the market to date. Man, I hope that's true. I can embrace my own hypocrisy, to an extent. But falling into a campsite with two charming farm ladies feels a little too (subconsciously) good to be true.

Now it's time to turn my attention to the ficklest female of them all.

The ocean.

•

The waves are big. Really big. Too big for me. I'm lucky. I make it back to shore, breathless. Thankful to be alive.

I turn and look back at the big boy sets. Daunting. Punishing. But not unrideable. Just unrideable by me.

A lull hits. I see some experts out at the other spot. Team Brolinas.

I can see Johnny, Liam and a few other dudes. Liam is actually an incredible surfer. The best of the crew. Such a weirdo. But watching him is hypnotic.

Who doesn't love an underdog.

•

Being blown out of the water by guys that surf better than I ever will? It's OK. I'm still ecstatic that I'm even trying. That I'll get out of my cozy bed and come out here and give it a shot.

But there's something bigger. Witnessing myself changing, I'm still fearful but more direct. My actions, they're more…swift? I dunno. It all started when I was in Australia, and I'm still filling out these new clothes.

It's both difficult and fascinating to watch yourself change. People don't change that much. Look at a little boy as an adult. Still curious, still mischievous. Maybe a bit tamed but you can still see it in his eyes. But people that experience trauma can change a lot. From docile to ferocious.

Even lethal.

I never would have guessed it would be me.

The more people I witness dying, the less it feels like a big deal.

Plus, let's face it; some people just need to go.

Still, I can't take my eyes off of Liam. He's incredible. In the water, he shuns the awkwardness he has on land. He connects.

Bolinas, CA
Photo: Liam, breaking through the fog, dropping into a bomb and cutting a clean line. Fearless.
@georgeous Even people we loathe sometimes do beautiful things.

•

Hmmm.

I keep chewing on the last few encounters with Team Brolinas. Two clearly non-local females with them. I can't shake it.

With all of those guys in the water, and the waves this good, I have time.

Leaving my wetsuit on, I pull the car key from the sleeve on my calf, put a towel over the seat and drive to the other break.

Both Johnny and Liam's pickups are there. I park behind a tree. The big white van is such a billboard. I sometimes use it as a landmark, when I'm in the water. Here, it's probably best kept out of sight.

I feel like an idiot, lurking around in my wetsuit. But it's a decent cover. I can always pretend I lost my key, if anyone asks.

Johnny's truck. A lot of clutter but nothing of substance. Other than a Russian to English dictionary. Overly ambitious?

Liam's truck.

Zip ties.

In plain view.

Plus an arm rest that's clearly familiar with them.

•

I need time to marinate on my discovery. I default back to the local ritual: head home, rinse wetsuit, find coffee.

I walk by Frankie's room. Gone. She rises early. Super early, every day. She takes a hike with an elderly neighbor's dog before surfing, building something and then doing the books at the bar.

Maya? She's reading a nine-hundred page novel, with a cat on her chest.

"Want coffee?"

"You're gonna drive?"

"Are you gonna get up and make it?"

She looks down at the cat. Pets it. resigns.

"Almond milk latte? With sugar?"

"Pretty please."

•

Raj is tending to his green onions. All is right in the world. I use Google translate to figure out how to say good day. It's so obvious, I feel like an idiot.

"Bonjour."

"Oui, Monsieur Georges!" Then he speaks really fast. All I hear is: *Au Bon Pain, Croissant, Gérard Depardieu?*

"I'm sorry, I don't speak French."

"Non?"

"Maybe ten words."

"But how'd you…?"

"At The Bookstore. You were reading *No Exit* in French. I love Sartre. Plus, wearing a cravat in Bolinas is a dead giveaway."

"Oui." He smiles. Able to laugh at himself.

"May I ask a favor?"

"Oui, chef."

"Tell me what the fuck is going on around here."

•

"Hey George! Want some eggs?" Frankie is picking fresh veggies from the yard. "And look! Our first homegrown jalapeno!" She holds it up. It's tiny and cute. But I don't care. I'm livid.

My lower jaw is restless—unsure when to start my diatribe.

I walk into the kitchen and throw the coffee I bought for Maya into the compost bin. Because it's empty. I bought coffees for the three of us. And drank them all at Raj's.

Maya is at the counter daydreaming, as is her way.

"What the fuck?"

She withdraws into her seat. But a tinge of her can tell that my outburst is not unfounded.

Frankie walks through the back door, all smiles.

"Look! One of the radishes made it! It'd taste terrible in a breakfast burrito, but let's slice it up for a mini appetizer!" The glimmer in her eyes fades, when she meets mine.

"Johnny and crew are trafficking young women? From Russia and Mongolia?"

They almost look relieved. But sad. Frankie drops her tiny bounty on the cutting board. The radish rolls listlessly onto the counter. She opens the fridge.

"You might want to have a beer."

"It's 8:30am. And I've still got to work today." A half-truth. But I'm angry, and it's all I can think of.

"You might want to have two."

6

"The Marine Highway System? From Alaska? It seems so inefficient."

"But it's slow. And therefore much less strictly monitored. Who wants to tote contraband on the slow boat over a week, when you can fly in five hours?" Frankie continues her editorial. "Some loser bros with a few desperate Russian brides? They fit right in."

"Yeah. It's way more discreet than you driving around in your creepy van."

"Hey, that's my house. Be nice." The fact that they're being so forthcoming calms me a bit. "They never run to the police?"

"One girl did. Once. But not anymore. The sheriff brought her right back. Can you imagine? I don't know what happened to her, but now, if they think they've got a runner, they do something so that she doesn't have any fight left."

"Like tie her up with zip ties?"

"Maybe. Why?"

"I saw. Liam's car. A grip of ties. Torn door handle."

"Oh my god. Those cocksuckers." Even though she's in the know, this descriptive detail hits Frankie hard. "That is fucking awful."

"Horrendous."

Maya is listening. Playing with her food. Frankie and I have both cleaned our plates. Maya's not taken a single bite. The behavior of a hyper-empathizer. I'm pleased, when she lifts her head to speak.

"Think about it. These girls are pretty but poor. Really poor. From broken homes. They've chosen some bleak hope—a job far away. Maybe cleaning houses of rich American's they've seen on TV. Even cleaning hotel rooms would like winning the lottery. So they make one poorly informed decision. Just one. But they pay for it. Forever. Ugh."

She goes back to staring at her food. Frankie picks it up.

"Getting tricked by Russian mobsters and then transferred to Bolinas surfer wannabe thugs? Things are looking up for them. And Team Brolinas? They probably treat them decently on the boat ride from Alaska down to Washington—fearful of alerting the Canadian authorities. It must feel like a honeymoon."

It's rude, but I'm starving.

"Are you going to finish that?"

"All yours." Maya pushes her plate an inch toward me, and Frankie reaches across to grab the untouched piece of radish. She pops it in her mouth, finishes chewing and swallows, before starting to talk again. The correct way to eat and converse.

"But once they reach Seattle? They fully turn them."

"Turn? Toward Bolinas?"

"Turn them into prostitutes."

•

The brutality is incomprehensible. Stolen passports. Disorientation. Intimidation. Gang rape.

How two organic farmers have kept this a secret, I have no idea.

•

Our breakfast is on hour two and may hit three.

"But why Bolinas? It's so invisible. So off the grid."

"That's exactly why." Maya says this and looks down at her hands. Either wishing she was hungry or wishing they'd chosen another town. Frankie finishes Maya's thought.

"Can you think of a more discreet pit stop?"

"Not really. If you were gonna traffic women, you've gotta stop somewhere? And somewhere with light visibility, so a port close to San Francisco is not an option. But a coastal spot with a volunteer-only police force? It's probably a no brainer."

"Bolinas."

•

Overwhelmed.

Desperate for distraction, I check emails. TR is a sight for sore eyes.

From: Rogers, Timothy

To: Lewis, George

Subject: RE: Be like water

George—

Regarding giving you writing advice—this is a really good question. I am more of a business unit manager than a content creative (like you), so I can only guide you from that lens. But I do have visibility into the mechanics of what gets published.

In short—keep doing what you're doing.

In long—the voice of your love advice vignettes was extremely raw, personal. The deviation you've offered up with the Novice Learns to Surf blurbs is different. It's aspirational and almost epistolary.

Do I personally think that "aspirational" is the voice the Creative Director will want applied to the surfing and/or Bruce Lee pieces? I have no idea. The only thing I know for sure is that whomever is assigned to oversee it will want their fingerprint on it. As a best practice, they always say to increase the tension and add theater, regardless of how dramatic a piece is. It's a bit obvious, kind of like telling someone to have a safe flight. But expect to hear it at least once, before you're done.

Just keep doing what you're doing. What's most important is that these pieces capture your experience—their core essence. Because ultimately, you will have to rewrite much of the content (as you have already experienced). So, it's critical that your first drafts can return you to that original feeling. If it does, it'll feel authentic. And you'll be able to morph it into something we might publish. If it doesn't? We'll cut it.

I hope that helps.

TR

P.S. Please never tell anyone that I gave you writing advice.

Wow. Didn't know TR had it in him.

I get in bed. But I'm still a bit edgy from the trafficking young women dialogue.

Grabbing *Maritime Law* as my laptop stand, I see a rip on the edge of the hardcover, where it attaches to the binding. I hate to think of duct taping over the beautifully embossed spine, but it's currently too valuable as a table. And from what I can see, the only enforcement of maritime law that will ever come from it will be throwing it at Johnny's smug face.

From: Lewis, George

To: Rogers, Timothy

Subject: Do you think your kung fu is, uh, better than mine?

Tim—

Thanks so much for your note. Very, very helpful.

I am having a bizarre day. Although every day is bizarre, here in

Bolinas.

Taking a swing at kung fu (no pun intended), see below. Based on your notes, I'm opting to continue with polished notes (possible overstatement) over complete pieces.

Bruce Lee #2

We do so many things to feel strong, safe, protected.
Exercise. Make money. Prepare for natural disasters.

All of these things help us feel secure. Not necessarily strong, but they make us feel less vulnerable.

As a male, the protective instinct is infused in us early. I was given my first toy gun at age four. A year before my first bicycle. One of my earliest memories is protecting my bike with the gun, from invisible adversaries.

This need, this desire to be strong, permeates our every action. From buying skinny jeans highlighting muscular quads to late night ads for testosterone supplements to our addiction to gladiator sports, like football.

Commerce, in its purest form, rarely seeks to create the best product. Instead, it uses shame to humiliate the consumer. Even commerce is fear-based.

But what's it like to directly address this fear? The fear of, "I'm afraid someone is going to hurt me. I'm afraid a big guy is going to intimidate me. Threaten me. I'm going to learn how to fight back."

Bruce Lee weighed one hundred and forty pounds. Less than my last girlfriend. But would you want to fight him?

That's the first thing I notice. Sparing with my teacher. Or Sifu. It's the first moment of my life I feel completely unafraid. Because fictitious or not—I'm preparing to meet my nemesis. And with each punch, kick and throw, I whittle away at this daunting tower of intimidation.

And that's why it makes so much sense. That Bruce Lee's Fists of Fury fueled this fear of being overcome by the bad guy. But Bruce Lee himself? He was calm. A philosopher. A healer. Because he addressed his demons, directly.

George Lewis
Staff Writer

Wow. Yet another rambling, incoherent piece of shit. But something is better than nothing. Always. And I'm too emotionally spent to clean it up.

Sleep.

•

6am.

Nothing has turned me into a morning person like sleeping in the van. A well-appointed van with a plush Tempur-Pedic mattress? It doesn't matter. It's still a car. Proof: my phone sleeps in a cupholder.

I know my wetsuit is still damp. How? Every time my arm escaped the covers last night, it got chased back underneath by the fog. Brrr.

I should rally and go surfing.

I should stop fantasizing about asking Maya if I can crawl into bed with her.

Cold, I doze back to sleep.

Knock, knock (lightly).

"George, you up?"

Frankie can see that I am.

"Wanna come in?"

She drops her board on some weeds and steps inside the van, closing the door behind her.

"It's cold!"

"I know. Here."

I toss her a blanket.

She grabs it and cocoons on the floor of the van—aka my three square foot living room. During the day, when I move the cooler six inches back and use it as a desk, it becomes an office.

"Oh my god. Oh my god. I should not have done that." Her voice is muffled in the blanket. "I'm so comfy." The floor has a small area rug that I bought at Bed Bath & Beyond. She probably is.

"I know." I nestle back into my bed. It's brisk enough to make my nose run.

"It is sooo cozy in here." She tucks herself in.

"Yeah, every breath is freezing. But the rest of my body feels like it's in a flannel hot tub of fantasticness." I pull the comforter up under my chin.

"Don't tempt me. Your bed looks even warmer than the floor." Is my micro-crush on the wrong person? Her voice is really growing on me. And I'm pretty sure she can read my mind, because she answers the question I'm thinking. "Tried to wake Maya. She's still asleep."

"I'm sure."

"How'd you know?"

"Because she follows you."

"Come on."

"It's true. I'm not saying she's not an independent thinker. She is. But you're the captain."

"Yeah. I'm a bitch."

I shimmy up in bed, so I can lean my head against the damp windowsill.

"No, you're not. You're just resolute. People like Maya? Maya is a soft touch. A pleaser. Like me. But even in your strength, you have a deep-seated vulnerability. It's sweet."

She ponders it.

Nope.

"Fuck this noise. Let's go surfing."

•

"That's better, but you've gotta move more. On a long board it's walking. A short board is rail-to-rail. But it's still the same. You wanna give the wave the most volume of the board to keep your speed up. Just bend your knees. Let the board tell you what it wants. Tell you where its sweet spot is."

"OK. OK. Jesus, I'm tired."

Frankie is grinding me out like a trophy-child parent at the gymnastics regionals. Unfortunately, the pounding surf in Bolinas is not nearly as predictable as the parallel bars.

"Pop up fast. Drive down the line. You can't be passive. If you try to follow the wave, it'll swallow you."

•

"Hey, can I borrow this?"

"You can have it. I have a spare."

She takes the barely used roll of duct tape and slides it over her wrist, like a bracelet for The Hulk.

"Sweet!"

"You talk like such a dude sometimes."

"At least one of us does."

"But your Sonicare regimen is so legit, whenever you say, 'rad' or 'sweet' your face lights up with that big smile."

"Shut up." She points to *Maritime Law*. "Why are you reading that?"

"I thought it was cool looking and apropos for our locale. But after twenty pages of the Admiralty Law distinction and the several dozen on convalescing seamen? It's now a bedside table. You'd think that Pirate Law would at least be exciting. Blue Beard, et cetera. No dice."

"Plus, you know it's all bullshit, right?"

"It's a thousand pages of 'thereforethingly' and 'aforementioned', so yes, I do."

"No, I mean as an effective legal statute. Think of every fucked up thing that's ever happened at sea. The guy that murdered his wife on their honeymoon on a Carnival Cruise? The frat boys that raped that girl during their Semester at Sea?"

"Yeah?"

"Why are none of them in prison?"

"Attorneys?"

"Not prosecuted. Maritime Law is so difficult to enforce and so vague on who has jurisdiction, no one bothers."

"Is that why you haven't done anything about Team Brolinas?"

"Who says I've done nothing?"

Bolinas, CA

Photo: Spine of Maritime Law, reduced to "time", due to duct taped edges.
@georgeous Time heals all (duct taped) wounds. Helpful assistance by:
@frankiethetankie

•

Smack, smack.

No one respects the tattered sign next to the screen door at the Bolinas People's Store: *Close me gently. I am old.* It's only complaint to constant abuse is a light squeak. A gracious sentry.

I'm out of toothpaste. The beauty of Bolinas? Zero choices. No frills Colgate it is. The pathway to peace is the absence of choice.

Heading to check out, three women walk in, each one younger than the next. Two of them are alabaster white and the third is Chinese…err, Mongolian. The oldest is twenty, tops. I wonder if I can gain their trust within ten seconds and make a run for it with them in the van.

"That all, darlin'?"

"Yeah, thank you. Do you guys sell the newspaper? I didn't see a rack."

"That one's free." She points to the *Bolinas Hearsay News*. She could be my grandma's little sister. If my grandma was a medicinal marijuana farmer.

"Uhm, I was thinking…"

"Just kiddin' yah. We've got yesterday's *San Francisco Chronicle*. You can have it. I always buy Thursday's for the funnies and the coupons. Crossword is too hard these days." Maybe she is my grandma?

"I'd love that. Thank you. You know what? Let me grab a bottle of wine real quick." The prices are ridiculous, but her kind gesture should not go unrewarded. Plus, I'm so bored. I might even read the Business section. I'd check the weather, but in Bolinas, it's on repeat: fog.

I grab a bottle and sneak a glance at Johnny's hostages. They're huddled around the toiletries. I can't pass by them nonchalantly with just the Pinot, so I grab a six pack from the cooler that's next to them. As I brush by, they're perusing the makeup section—aka two mascaras, three eye thingies and a concealer. The two Russians watch me from their periphery, not turning their heads. The Mongolian woman, who is really more of a girl, shoots me a curious glance. It either says: *Help me* or *Do you think I'm pretty?* She's so sad and abused, she might not know the difference.

Smack.

The door announces Johnny's abrupt arrival. Holding a grip of cash, he beats me to the cash register.

"Heeey, Regina." The fake drawl is back. He thinks he's Matthew McConaughey. He glances down the makeup aisle, approvingly. They started hurrying the moment he entered. He nods to tell them to finish up.

"Well alright, alright."

OK, his McConaughey is pretty good.

Regina has set the dog-eared Chronicle next to the register. I drop the Pinot and KSAs on the counter. Johnny welcomes me with a greasy forefinger on the front page: *Cal Bears upset UCLA Bruins.*

"You still here? Ain't it time to get back to SoCal?" He doesn't say *Professor*, with his fictitious twang, and I'm disappointed. But he does chomp his gum like an unaware fifth grader. It's the small things.

"Did you go to college in the south? Bama?" Regina, sensing our rivalry, takes a few steps away from us. But she stays close enough to listen.

"Nah." He doesn't like this line of questioning. Glares at the three of them to hurry up.

"Can't quite place your accent. Louisiana? Sorry, I've not traveled much."

"Ladies?" Johnny deflects, trying to disengage.

I nod to Regina. She returns to the register, reluctantly.

"Forty-eight thirteen." Holy expensive bottle of red.

"Memphis? What's the school there?" I'm confident he'll say some Cali school, and I'm pretty excited about it.

Regina slides my change across the counter and retreats to her corner.

"Went to Humboldt for a bit."

Bingo.

Humboldt may be a little hillbilly, but it's still in California. Below the Mason-Dixon line it's not.

"Gotcha. Pretty spot." I don't even need to condescend.

How does he regain his male dominance? He pops his gum, pulls it out of his mouth and sticks it on my newspaper.

Classy.

"Girls. Let's go."

Johnny drops a crisp hundred-dollar bill next to the cash register. A hundred. In Bolinas. And he motions them out. They comply.

Regina foregoes the register and whisks the Franklin into her pocket. She shakes her head at Johnny's gum, gingerly folds a corner over it, rips it off and throws it away. A small gesture but it's got a lot of heart.

"Don't mind him, darlin'. Chip on his shoulder. And the paper's still fine! Just a little nibble out of it!"

"Yeah, like a nibble from a rattlesnake."

•

Driving out of downtown, the road dips toward the farm, before turning toward Highway 1 and on to San Francisco.

I see Maya walking toward me, at half speed. Aka Bolinas speed.

"Hey there."

"Where're you walking to?"

"Downtown. Off today. Was going to have a long lunch. Read a book."

She taps the chest pocket of her jacket, with a paperback outline. I'm envious of the book's proximity to…

"You?"

"SF. Kung fu class."

"For realsies? I thought that was a joke?"

"Nope. For real. Is that something I would joke about?"

"Yeah, but you're always doing your deadpan thingie. Frankie and I never believe a word you say."

"Sorry, that sucks. The straight man bit? I'm so used to no one laughing at my jokes, I pretty much just say them for myself."

"Poor baby."

"Do you wanna come?"

"To San Fran?"

"Yeah. But don't call it that. It makes you sound like you're from LA or, gasp, Phoenix."

"Oh, right."

"Maybe I'm being overly self-conscious. Us LA apologists—the shame runs deep." She half-smiles. Either not getting my joke or not thinking it was funny.

She pops in the passenger side.

"Giddy up!"

Redemption. Only people I really like use this phrase.

•

"Can you ask Frankie if you guys need anything for the farm or the bar?"

"I already have a list on my phone. Frankie asked me to grab some fertilizer and stuff at Lowe's or Home Depot, when we went to Fort Point. It just seemed a bit much to ask, since you drove four kegs back."

"Really? I don't care. I'd love to help. Even in some teeny way, like big box store errands. Let's get it today. Where's The Depot?"

"Not that close. There's one in Corte Madera and another south of the city. Lowe's is closer, but they don't have as big of a nursery."

"What are you gonna do, while I'm becoming a badass?"

"Read in a coffee shop?"

"Take the van to the nursery? You'd be doing me a favor. Parking this thing in Nob Hill is brutal."

"Really? You'd be OK with that?"

"Of course."

"But this is your house?"

"If you crash, I'll move into your house. Win/win."

7

Like a Chihuahua riding an elephant, I see her little chocolate forehead above the steering wheel, lumbering up the hill. She double parks, unsure of what to do.

"You've been waiting long?"

"Nah, I had to take some notes, and I was starving. They're closed now, but I have a room temperature cold brew for you in my bag, if you want it?"

"I'd prefer a glass of wine. And for you to drive. Starting now. This thing is a beast."

I jump in and drive a few blocks, pulling over in a yellow zone.

"Gimme two minutes? I just want to get the rest of this down." I pull a pen from my pocket.

"Of course! Oh my god. I'm so glad not to be driving." She furrows her brow. "Is your lip swollen?"

"It's fine. I mistakenly blocked a punch with my face."

I grab my notebook and write quickly, attempting to close it out. The vignette I've been scribbling for the last hour.

Bruce Lee #3

"Pick up the black gloves and foot guards."

"OK?"

"Today, we're going to spar."

"Against you?"

"Yes."

"Uhhh."

"We'll start slow. Follow me."

I do. We warm up. It's falsely reassuring. We're at twenty percent speed, so I'm blocking most of his shots. But his tempo builds.

Punch.

"Ow!"

Kick.

"Ow!"

"Blocking is not enough. Every time your opponent strikes, he leaves himself open,

exposed. You must treat every act of aggression as an opportunity."

I shuffle my feet and regroup. Block a few kicks. Then I take a swing. He flicks it away, effortlessly.

"React. Block. Respond."

He slows down. Throwing ultra-low-speed kicks and punches.

"React. Block. Respond."

He continues. I stay silent.

"Again."

"React. Block. Respond."

"Again."

"Practice until it becomes one movement. Practice until an act of aggression feels like a gift."

He speeds up.

Punch.

My lip splits.

Finishing the last line, I instinctively lick my swollen, split lip.

It absolutely did not go down like that. But I'm confident *Esquire* would not publish the actual story:

"Hey buddy! You game to do a little sparring? We'll go slow, I promise!"

And thank god he's like this, because it completely dissolves the intimidation. Especially since he's wearing baggy sweatpants I've seen at Costco for $9. In full transparency—I have an indestructible down parka from Costco, and it's saved my bacon more than once.

Ding. He pops me.

"Ow!"

"Sorry kiddo! I thought you were gonna block it!"

"So did I."

"I didn't mean to! You were really getting the hang of it!"

"No worries. My fault. The punishment fits the crime."

"Ooof! It's all red! Let me get the blue ice from my lunch bag!"

•

"Where do you wanna go?"

"It's so hard to park this thing, I usually just go wherever I find a spot."

"Oh my god. Driving the hills in this thing scared me to death."

"Me too. But I'm getting used to it." We crest a hill. The van feels like it's going to roll backwards, unstoppably, into a high-rise. "Let's head toward the other side of Nob Hill. Worst case, I know a garage. We can go to the spot I went last time—*Dunya*. It's awesome."

I make a few turns.

"Holy shit, it reeks of fertilizer."

She looks over her shoulder at her shopping binge.

"Sorry, Frankie wanted to try out a few new ones. The Bolinas fog, you know?"

"I do."

"Plus, I couldn't resist your huge, nearly empty van at Home Depot."

"I know the feeling."

"Spot! Spot!"

She points to a miracle on Hyde street. A spot with a driveway in front—no need to parallel park. Victory.

"Perfect. Thank you."

"*Cafe Meuse?* Wanna go there?" Maya points diagonally to a quintessential San Francisco wine bar. Hyde Street is hilly and full of trees. The bar is tucked in a corner awning, beneath a hundred-year-old Victorian. Or Edwardian. I don't know the difference. We may not be on a date, but it sure feels like one.

She reaches up and touches my chin, underlining the scab on my lip with her thumb.

"Your coach hits you?"

"Really softly."

"Maybe you need a new coach?"

"Nah, just someone to kiss it and make it better." After hearing it said aloud, I grimace. "Sorry. I hate myself for saying that. That was dumb."

"You're so silly sometimes!" She kisses her fingers and gently taps my lips. On the side, away from the cut. Carefully.

"You could be a professional at taunting."

"Because you let me. You know who you should be chasing?"

"No one. Truly. I'm still a man and have…desire? But it doesn't matter. The last few months have been an emotional tornado. I'm taking a breather. Or at least trying to."

"That's how everyone feels all the time."

"Really?"

"Yep."

"That's terrible."

"It's just a fact. And it's not the fact that's important, it's how you deal with it."

"Wow. Can I steal that?"

"Huh?"

"That line. For work. It's great."

"Sure. Whatever. But I was trying to say that you should date Frankie."

"Why?" Although I already know the answer. Because Frankie is great. But it's a weird sales pitch. "Especially from a woman that gave me a kiss in an industrial refrigerator, when she didn't need to."

"Because she's the best person I know."

"That's a really beautiful compliment."

"She deserves it. And I don't deserve you."

"I'm not that nice."

"I didn't say you were. But you are attentive. And you're trying. That's a lot. For a guy."

"The compliment stings a little, but I'll take it."

"That's exactly what I mean. You will take a back-handed compliment and not push. Not obsess. It's so…unusual…in boys. No offense."

"I'm just lucky to get to spend this time with you two. It's really great. And I'm appreciative. Platonic is not a synonym for failure."

"True. It's not. It just never ends up that way."

We've been standing outside the wine bar for a few minutes. A cordial barman cracks the door and pops his head out. He knows he's interrupting something, and he knows he might be saving us. I'm thankful.

"You know you guys can come inside! We've been open for ten minutes!"

I turn to Maya.

"Can you get us a table? I wanna grab my sweater. Just got a chill."

"For sure."

And the relationship talk I'm having with the person that I'm not in a relationship with is over.

•

You know when you can't find your keys in your house, even though the house is spotless? The van is equally as hard to find anything—it's almost too well organized. Searching for my dressiest clothing option, a plain grey sweater, requires that I shift Maya's purchases a few inches. Five small bags of fertilizer. Six gallons of Drano. Gallons. A restaurant sized roll of tin foil. A few other things that don't seem like necessities for a farm. Unless you're harvesting homemade explosives.

•

Taking a few whiffs of my sweater to confirm it doesn't smell like Miracle-Gro, I walk back in. Maya is all smiles. She sips her glass, and she's ordered me a light colored beer. I grab it without toasting.

"They don't have KSA, but they had another Fort Point beer. I just got that, 'cause you're kind of a fan boy."

"Perfect."

Gulp, gulp.

I settle into the seat. She's backed off our little spat and is enjoying herself. But behind every smile is yet another secret.

"Karate must've made you so thirsty!"

"Kung fu." I set the beer down. Almost empty. Maya senses my stoicism. She's glad to see the friendly barman approach.

"Another round for you two?"

"Yes, please!"

He nods, like opting for another round is the best indicator that a date is going well. A nod he's given a thousand times. Fair enough. This is a dream spot for an online date.

Maya toasts me. She doesn't wait for me and takes a sip. The barman must've chosen well, as she does a little happy-dance in her seat.

"Yum, yum, yum! This is so nice! In the city. The trees. A quiet spot. A glass of Sauvignon blanc...a handsome man..." She giggles.

I roll my eyes.

She gives a slight frown but doesn't deny it.

Our drinks arrive. Because I'm driving, I know this one is my last. But I still pound it.

We lock eyes. We're having a moment. Well, at least one of us is. If we were on an actual date, this would be a perfect time to lean over and kiss her. And not that bullshit fridge kiss. A real one. This locale has completely changed her demeanor. But her coy flirtation isn't enough. I'm too wound up.

"So where'd you learn your bomb-making skills?" Probably not my best timing. But I want to put her on the spot, while Frankie's not here to protect her. "Who buys two pound bags for a four acre farm? A fucking farm? It's like bringing a ketchup packet to the Hot Dog Eating Finals."

"Gross!" She starts laughing. But then her smile turns sad.

•

By our fifth round, we're either getting a hotel or waiting until 3am, when I can drive. It's turned into a one-sided confessional. Me asking about what is going on in Bolinas. Her revealing a little bit about herself. Grazing her secrets. Me keeping mine.

She takes another sip and takes a deep breath. Preparing to conclude what little she was willing to share.

"I grew up having decisions made for me. And they were bad, bad decisions. Ugh. Yuck. So I started making my own. But I just ended up going from one sucky situation into another."

•

Maya walks through her life since being a teen. Getting a lot of unwanted attention from men. Never trusting them. But she never says anything concrete. Just vagaries. She also doesn't relate her own experiences as a prologue to what's going on in Bolinas. She lets me fill in the cracks and come to that conclusion myself.

Our thoughts jump around. But mine always return to our shared north bay town.

Another grazing of stories. This time, not her own.

Some clarity. At least for me.

"Ohhh, so that's why they were buying makeup? For the rendezvous at sea?"

"Yeah."

"And your bomb-making kit also RSVP'd to the event?"

"That's Frankie's idea. Way too scary for me."

"No doubt."

•

"This whole thing, it makes me want to kill myself." I shake my head and take another swallow.

"I know. You're not alone. Not even close. It's so, so icky."

•

Our intuitive barman returns, almost fearfully, having witnessed our rollercoaster of emotions from behind the bar. But he can also tell that we have something. And he doesn't want to break the spell. Genuine empathy for total strangers. Rarer than a red diamond.

Maya and I, drunk as idiots, have been holding hands across the table for an hour. It's 11pm. We are druuunk.

"It's last call. We close early on weeknights. Are you guys…?"

"Nah, we're all set. Thanks."

"Do you sell halvsie glasses?"

"We do!"

"And a beer for him?"

"Absolutely!"

Maya gets very excited about ordering half drinks.

He walks away, and I want to lie down on the floor.

"Maya. I'm fucking taco'ed. Neither of us can drive. And you just got another round?"

He drops our drinks. Maya hands him a debit card, before I can say: *chivalry*. Or at least slur it.

Maya takes a sip of her Sauvignon blanc, sets it down and spider-crawls her fingers up my arm. Tenderly. Suggestively.

Her nearly-black hair compliments her skin. I challenge my initial observation that her skin is the color of chocolate milk. It is, for sure. But it has different consistencies. More like when you make chocolate milk from Nesquik powder to control the strength. A little different every time. But always sweet. And a little curious.

"Why do you care? So much?"

"About this fucked up situation?"

"Yeah. It's not really your problem."

"That passiveness—it's actually super dangerous. I've witnessed people dying due to passivity. Or maybe it's incompetence? I dunno. I guess it's OK when it's criminals that get hurt. But victims do, too. I just...I dunno...it unnerves me."

"Yeah...letting things happen, even to ourselves, it can be so harmful. It just feels...nasty, right?"

"Indeed."

"Plus, passive criminals can be victims, too."

•

7am.

It's my second night waking up on the streets of San Francisco. Next time? I'll park somewhere flatter. Maya is lying across me due to our physicality and also gravity.

My lips are chapped from dehydration and a thirty-minute make out. A small portion of it spent on her deep brown left nipple—the full extent of our disrobing, while parked steeply downhill on Hyde Street.

She falls asleep really, really fast.

I check the sign through the big van window—street cleaning starts at 9am. I have time. I disentangle from my almost lover.

Getting dressed when you've slept in your pants? Also really fast.

Maya's bra? It's dusted with fertilizer from lying on the floor. I blow it clean, and the smell wafts up. Ooof.

She rolls over.

I tuck her in and cover her bare shoulder with her own top. In case she wakes up looking for it. The tint on the van windows could be a little darker.

"Stay here. I'm gonna grab coffee."

She mumbles an affirmative and then immediately pulls the blanket up over her face.

•

My walk down to the merchant district is its own shot of espresso. Steep and crisp and eye opening. San Francisco in the early morning is the prettiest damn city I've ever seen.

"Fuck."

Nope.

Shit.

Human shit. I scrape it off my shoe with the curb. That's how I know I've hit Polk Street.

San Francisco, CA
Photo: The sun dancing over Nob Hill and Pacific Heights, with the street and its trash framed at the bottom.
@georgeous Yet another city where you have to step over a homeless person to get into a Maserati dealership. @sf_mayor

I pass a handful of $50 manicure/pedicure spots and a lot more homeless. So much wealth, yet nowhere for the poor to use a bathroom. This may be one of the richest cities in the world, but the price of dignity is still too high.

•

I try to be as quiet as possible. But breakfast burritos + coffees + 160lb van door = not a subtle way to wake up Maya. I got a waffle, too.

"I got you an almond milk latte."

"Ugh."

"And some food."

"Ugh. So hungover."

"Shall I just drive us back to Bolinas? You can stay in bed and sleep more."

"That would be amazing."

"But you have to fully indemnify me if we crash. There's no seatbelt back there."

No response. Her face returns under the blanket.

I eat the waffle first.

•

"Netflix DVDs? In the mail-back-sleeve?" I point to it.

"Welcome to 2004 and present day Bo." Frankie fans her face with the red sleeve.

Their mailbox is a solid quarter mile from the house, on a dirt road. Her outfit is the equivalent of running out to grab the paper on the driveway, if the driveway is made of rocks, sparse weeds and is eight blocks away.

"Wow. Just wow."

"Bobo is so stuck in time, I've looked into getting a Redbox for the bar. It would kill, and we could use the profits to pay for a sturdier lockbox—to replace the one we keep confiscated knives in." She's not kidding.

"That's insane. Then why not? The Redbox?"

"Some fucker here would steal it, in the back of his pickup truck, just for sport."

"Where's the Bolinas Border Patrol, when you need them?"

"Who do you think brings knives to the bar?"

Frankie looks around the inside of the van. She's wearing Ugg boots, short shorts and a hoodie. Her hair is up in a messy bun. In this light, it's the color of a burnt foxtail. And there might be one hiding up in it, but she wouldn't bother to pull it out. She might think she looks her absolute worst. More likely, she doesn't care. My opinion? She looks perfect. Love triangles always sound terrible, until you're in one.

"Do you have my roommate in there?"

She can already see her lumpy shape, face down in the bed.

"Yeah, we…"

She interrupts me with a finger. Then uses it to unlock her phone. Shows me a text from last night at 10:30pm:

George's forearms are so long and veiny. I wonder if his penis looks like that?

My jaw drops but pauses half way. Why? Because she's covering up how she responded with her hand.

She advised me against hooking up with Maya. But her sharing this nugget with me suggests that she's not mad. Or maybe she, too, is curious? Male egocentricity is bottomless.

"I got the New York Times, see?" I grab it, flex my forearm and smirk.

She hops in for the short ride back. After slamming the door, she flicks the big vein on my wrist. Hard.

•

Frankie drinks what's left of Maya's coffee and doesn't balk at it being cold. Tough. Endearing.

Uh oh.

This is a disaster. I need to get out of this town before I do something stupid. Stupider than last night.

I guess it's because even the most mundane of interactions with Frankie—a ride down the dirt driveaway—feel so natural. She makes the small moments so effortless.

There's also something about Frankie that makes me truly trust her. Maybe it's her strength. I don't know. I'm gonna make her tell me her secret about the fertilizer. Which she will. And I will probably tell her my secrets. Which I shouldn't. Something I didn't even consider last night with Maya.

We get a few hundred feet from the house, and Maya is still passed out.

Frankie is rummaging through the breakfast burrito remains, pinching at a bit of egg and tortilla.

"Shall I drop the bomb-making supplies at the barn? Or were you guys planning to construct the igniter in the kitchen?"

•

"Your plan has so many flaws."

"Because you're the expert in subterfuge?"

"Compared to you two?"

•

It's been just the two of us for about an hour.

So I tell her.

Everything.

Everything, everything.

"Your old boss in Panama sold guns to terrorists and killed your best friend, who had a love child that had a pedophile guardian that you helped execute? And now you want to learn to surf and try to get karate articles printed in a magazine?"

"It feels incredibly oversimplified, in your summary, but yes. That's the gist of it."

"Damn, George. Maybe you're more qualified than I thought."

8

"So you blow up Johnny's boat. Never mind that fertilizer bombs and all of your other strategies are absurd. Then what?"

"Disable the boat, George. Not blow up. Disable." She corrects me. But it sounds like a joke. As if she was underlining the word *disable* with a pen made of sarcasm.

"With a bomb?"

"Maybe a small one? We don't want to rule anything out."

"Like what?"

"Cutting the fuel lines. Sabotaging the electrical. That's where we're leaning."

"I love how you talk about it like you're picking an accent color for a bedroom."

"We're not fucking around, George."

"I know. I know. I'm honestly impressed you're so matter of fact about it. But won't Johnny just fix the boat? What's the real gain, other than creating hassle for him and giving him a reason to come after you?"

"That's true. He probably will." These are the first words out of Maya's mouth. Her demeanor suggests: *I'm on this bus, because it's the right thing to do. But my heart's not in it.*

"No! Not probably!" Frankie gives her a firm look. "We disable the boat. By the easiest and safest means, with a few backup options. Then we radio the Coast Guard."

"But there's no way they'd host a party on a boat that's dead in the water. They'd certainly not bring their ladies there."

"Exactly. The whole plan is to scoop the girls. It doesn't even matter if the Coast Guard comes. Johnny and crew will be monitoring that channel. They'll hear the distress call referencing their own boat. We're just trying to fuck with them. Get them off their game. Grab the girls and get them to the consulate."

"One of his other bros is just gonna hand them over to you?"

"George. Seriously. Do you think I've not thought this through?"

"Sorry. But...how?"

"After the Coast Guard, we call the Sheriff's Department. Homeland Security. If I have to, I'll call the DEA and say that the guy that sold the fentanyl to Prince is on that fucking boat. They've got Marin County Sheriff's Department in their pocket, and they'll alert Team Brolinas to all of the unwanted attention. They'll drop the girls like a sack of hammers."

"Yeah. Huh. That's actually a pretty good plan."

•

I've adopted an end-of-the-day relaxation ritual where I sit on the van's floor/living room and close out the day. Send a few emails. Sip a beer. Think.

But it doesn't always work.

Restlessness. My most adamant suitor.

Click, click.

An impulse buy at REI, I unfold the Eno Hammock and hook the carabineers onto the back rear and side door bars. The installation only takes two seconds, which is why I bought it.

I try to convince myself that it's comfortable. It's not quite right. It's missing something. A longer van or a shorter inhabitant.

"George?"

"Hey."

Maya's carrying two beers. Bummer. Because if it was four, I'd know that she was considering another sleepover. Her loungey outfit says she could go either way.

"That looks…"

"I know. It's a work in progress."

"Why don't you hang one end on the fence? Then you won't be so…diagonal?"

"Yeah, but I like it inside. Sort of a fort within a fort. You know?"

"I guess. Can I try?"

Her small frame fits perfectly.

•

"I'm gonna go."

"Do you wanna stay?"

"I figured after last night…you'd assume you can start staying in my bed."

"Of course not."

"Really?"

"We drunk kissed in my van. I don't think that qualifies as an intimacy accelerator." I wait a second, but she doesn't take the bait. "Maya…"

"I'm shy."

•

We're both in the hammock. Damn this thing is strong. There's so much blood constriction in my leg that it's fallen asleep. The struggles of semi-prone cuddling.

Always fantastic at letting sleeping dogs lie, I've asked her again, about why she split with Johnny.

"I left Phoenix to get away from a life I didn't want. I wanted a change. I'd seen Bolinas in one of those AAA magazines."

"There was a piece on Bolinas in *Via*? No way."

"Yep. It seemed like the exact opposite of Phoenix. So quiet. And remote."

"It is."

"Kinda. But when you move, the last thing you pack is everything you hate about yourself, so you don't have to buy it again, when you get there."

"Too true."

"I met Johnny after being here a week. I was homesick. He

reminded me of home. Maybe a little too much."

•

Bolinas, CA—Dodge van interior
Photo: Bedding crammed into the hammock.
@georgeous Cohabitating in a hammock is like taking a nap on fake breasts. It sounds comfortable, until you try it. @enohammocks

If it weren't for the ocean calling my name, I'd wake Maya and have us drop down seven inches onto my actual bed and sleep for three more hours. But it's time to get wet.

•

From: Lewis, George
To: Rogers, Timothy
Subject: Dawn Patrol

TR—

Apparently, I am turning into a morning person.

1. You've got to try surfing. It's so awesome.
2. Latest Life Skills (semi) polished notes pasted below.
3. My makeshift campsite has inconsistent WiFi. I often tether my phone to my computer to send you these emails. I just want to make sure that I don't overdo it on the bill. A free cellphone is a tremendous luxury. I don't want to lose the privilege.

Best,

George

Surfing #3

*I've heard dozens of people say, "It gives me a reason to get up in the morning."
And I thought they were all cliché-spewing idiots. But surfing makes it all make
sense.*

*Visualize a metaphor. There's a female. She's gorgeous but in an offbeat way. Her
sister must endorse every guy she dates. And she's only free once a week, for an hour
after church.*

*That's how many variables are involved in finding good waves. The three main
things? Tide, wind and swell.*

The tide is her body. Oftentimes too skinny. Rarely too thick.

*The wind is her face. Is it smooth like milk? Or tormented by too many years spent
in bars.*

*The swell is the most important. It's her temperament. Her emotions. Is she a
cutter, insightful but biting? Or a confident woman at peace, quick to smile, with
perfectly balanced vibrancy, ferocity and calm.*

In the time it takes me to rinse out my wetsuit, he's already
responded.

From: Rogers, Timothy
To: Lewis, George
Subject: Dawn Patrol

George—

Nice to see you in my inbox before lunch. Sadly, once you've practiced surfing and had a cup of coffee, I've already been on three conference calls and had a staffer miss a deadline. Jealousy is an ugly thing.

To your questions:

1. I took a surfing lesson while on vacation in Morocco. It was way too hard. Casablanca was meant for boozy room service and Bogart movies, not extreme sports.

2. Keep them coming. I appreciate you giving me the first glance.

3. Phone bills: it's fine while you're traveling on assignment. But don't exceed $300 in a billing cycle. If you do, walk into an AT&T store, pay your monthly bill in cash, and we'll figure out how to reimburse you later (a handful of Uber rides, etc.). Exceeding that threshold requires me to go up three floors for approval. And you don't want me to do that. Trust me. I once submitted a $600 cell phone bill after returning from Iceland. Huge mistake. A story for another time.

4. I see a lot of relationship parallels in your newer pieces. Especially today's. The swell is her temperament? I'm not criticizing. It just suggests a bit of romantic torment.

5. Please don't respond to #4.

George, please stop worrying about the quality of your work. Just keep chugging along, and be pleased with the progress. Quality is very subjective. But progress? We have folks out on the road who don't submit a single paragraph for weeks. You're doing just fine.

TR

•

My coffee from Coast Cafe is still too hot. I tidy up the van, while I wait for it to cool.

Running my palm along the duct taped spine of *(Mari)time (Law)*, I decide to walk to The Bookstore.

"Monsieur Raj, bonjour."

"Ravi de vous voir mon ami!" At least I know what *mon ami* means.

"So, you do work here."

He turns toward me, but not all the way. A vintage fedora obscures his left eye. It's covered in makeup.

"Non, non. I run an AirBnB. The bookstore? I look after it for my friends. Keep an eye on it for them."

"Hopefully not your left eye."

•

Like me, Monsieur Raj can drink his bodyweight in coffee. When I return with his cafe au lait, he's already emptied the double espresso he was sipping earlier. He grabs the cup thankfully and adds half of a Stevia. Yes, they have Stevia in Bolinas.

We all play very specific roles with our friends. Unfortunately, this perpetuates our friends viewing us uni-dimensionally. And this is a tremendous loss. Because it's always inaccurate and insufficient. For example, my mother sees me as her hyper-sensitive, wayward son. By contrast? Monsieur Raj sees me as a cowboy. Reckless. Irreverent. I like the way the Stetson fits. For now.

"That makeup looks like shit."

"I've used it for blemishes several times; it always works fine."

"The fact that you said 'blemishes' says it all."

He looks quizzical. I drop it.

"I was moving a stack of misplaced biographies to…"

"Enough. Stop. Those knuckle marks across your eyebrow? They came from a fist. Who?" He drops his head, letting the fedora shade his eye. "You look like Panama Jack, without the monocle."

"I do?!"

He takes this as a compliment.

He deflects by scanning the fiction section. I follow, because it's what I came here to do, anyway. I see Lydia Millet's *Fight No More*. A brilliant read and a title that doubles as advice for my love life.

"Raj. Talk to me."

•

Frankie is home. Maya is not. No wonder love triangles are so exhausting.

"Is that for Maya?"

"It's for you?"

"Yeah, right." A poorly executed lie on my part. But she grabs the coffee anyway. "Your wetsuit is dry. I just turned it right side out. It's on the bannister."

"That's wonderful, thank you. You're so thoughtful."

"For a chick?"

"For anyone."

"Sometimes I wish you would just talk like a dude."

"Sometimes I do."

She smiles.

"You're smarter than you look." She looks out the window at the trees. "The wind hasn't kicked up. High tides isn't until four. That northwest swell is still cranking. I'm gonna paddle out. Wanna come?"

"Yeah...Uh..." I look at her. Hard. She doesn't flinch. She just wants to go surfing. And finish the coffee that wasn't bought for her. "Raj? Have you seen him? His face?"

"Raj? Maybe two days ago. I'm not a big reader. As you know, the best books come out as movies." She giggles, gritty with her raspy voice.

"Liam kicked the shit out of him."

"What! Why?"

"He wouldn't rent his AirBnB out to them. For their sex-cruise clients. Some low level guys from Silicon Valley that want to sleep with hotties but can't pull them by building iPhone apps and banking stock options."

"Motherfuckers."

She finishes her coffee, reaches under her shirt and unsnaps her bra—sliding it through her baggy t-shirt and laying it over the back of the couch.

"Follow me."

•

Frankie is muscular. She lifts her arm up. Points to the weaknesses in Johnny's boat. I catch a quick glimpse of her breast. Then quickly shake it off my mind. She removed her bra for this?

"How do you have this?"

"Amazon Prime. Half the town gets theirs delivered to the bar."

"You Amazon Primed electrical and fuel line blueprints to a poor man's luxury boat?"

"Yep. And razors. The ones they sell at the store carve up my legs. See?" She shows me.

"They look just fine. Insecure about your body, you are not."

"Nope." She smiles, satisfied with herself. And, at this point, I'm pretty confident she didn't take off her bra for me.

I look back at the drawings.

"The easiest places to reach look like here and here." I point.

"But you're right next to the galley. In full view. That's where they'll have pregame drinks, before the girls come."

"Come? How?"

"By boat. By another boat."

"Ahh." We stare at the blueprints for a bit. She makes a few markings with a pencil, so they can be erased. I point to a spot. "I see a weakness. The fuel from there. The propane from there. Right?"

"Right but wrong. See that?" She points to different view of the same area. "They're both only reachable under water, dipshit."

"Dipshit? Nice."

"Um, you're adding zero value, and you keep checking out my tits."

"Caught. But you took your bra off!"

"To put on my wetsuit, jacktard!"

"Oh. Right."

•

"OK. Let's do it. I wanna do it."

"You're gonna go underwater and cut two lines. Then get away without getting caught or hurt?"

"Yep."

"How?"

"I'm not sure yet."

"You're a fucking idiot."

"Maybe. But I'm already on my way out of here. If you do this, what are you gonna do? Where are you gonna go? You can't stay here."

"I know. I'm gonna go home. To Buellton. Winter is slow season. No weddings. I usually do a big snowboarding trip. Being away is not unexpected. The owner of Smiley's likes to spend a few weeks here a year, anyway. Make sure we haven't burned the bar down. She's happy to pull a few weeks of shifts, before taking off somewhere tropical to manage us from afar. Laura. She'll be here in a few days."

"What about Maya?"

"She'll come with me. At least she said she would."

"OK. Good."

"I'd do anything for that girl. Anything. But I can't save her from everything."

"Like?"

"Herself."

9

Maya is making tea from the mint that grows in the garden. It seems absurdly labor intensive, but the smell is amazing. Instead of boiling water, I wish she was opening a bottle of rum.

"Frankie left *Bronson* for us."

"That sleeper Tom Hardy movie?"

"I think so. The title is weird."

"We could just hangout."

"Anything. Watching a movie sounds lovely."

Other than Laura, the constantly traveling owner, and one other part-timer, Maya and Frankie alternate at the bar. It's a cool rhythm. Especially getting each of them all to myself. Maya continues futzing around in the kitchen. Looking but not finding.

"Do you want a beer?"

"I think we're out."

"Nah, I got more. And a bottle of red."

"Cab?"

"Yep."

"We've trained you well."

She gives my shoulder a light squeeze.

It's just enough.

She quarter turns, and I put a hand on her waist. Not pulling her back to me but suggesting that she does.

"Can I give you one real kiss? Stone cold sober. One legit kiss."

"Uhhh, sure?"

"Jesus. I can't believe I have to coax you into it." But her ambivalent verbal response doesn't stop her from leaning up toward me.

I kiss her. A little nervous at first. But she is too. I keep my left hand on her waist and run my right up over her shoulder. I rub it, lightly. Can feel how tense it is. The desire to pull away. But she lets go. Brings her hands up. Along my back. Scratching lightly. First up. Then down. She reaches my hips and then slides her hands in, toward my spine. Pulling me closer.

I pick her up. She pauses for a second, then wraps her legs around me. I walk two steps and push her against the hallway wall. Gently.

"George." It's almost a whisper.

She's seated in my arms like a swing set, and I lift her up. Kiss her neck. The top of her chest.

"George, just. Just one sec."

I pull back. Lock eyes with her.

"OK?"

"And uh, set me down?"

"Oh, yeah. Sorry."

"No. It's OK. I like it. It's just…Frankie told me. About the boat stuff."

"I figured. It saves me so much time with you guys catching up in between shifts."

"Really? I'd think most guys would hate it."

"True. It's awful. But it has some merit." She doesn't laugh.

"George. You can't. You can't do this." I have half an erection, and she could mean a lot of things. "You don't need to be the hero. Don't need to save us. We don't need that. And I don't want the guilt, honestly."

"Save you?"

"You can just leave Bolinas. You're here on vacation. You're not obligated to…"

"I'm not here on vacation."

"Whatever. It's not your job."

I kiss her. Because I can't think of what else to do. She's into it. But she breaks it off.

"OK. But I'm not doing this for you guys. I'm doing it for me."

"Zero percent?"

"OK. Not zero percent."

"See?"

"I'm doing it because it's the right thing to do. I'm doing it for me. Johnny? It has to stop. It's that simple." I keep my eyes locked on hers.

"Have I grown attached to you and Frankie? Of course. It's only been a little more than a week. You two are wonderful. Of course I am protective. But it's more than that. Way more."

She's not buying it. I've gotta go deeper.

"You don't even live here. This is a Bolinas thing."

"It's an everywhere thing."

"Huh?"

"My best friend died because I was a spectator. A month later? His brother? He stepped up and made sure my goddaughter has a future that is safe. He was willing to take control. Be decisive." I think for a moment about Craigo. I miss him. And I will forever be in his debt for being a proxy for PJ. It feels insincere to say another (even if it is his brother) scratches the itch of missing someone else. But Craigo did just that. So, so well. And the amount I have missed PJ—it's inconceivable.

"But you…"

"Yeah. I was there. Was I helpful? Yes. Was I decisive? No."

"But you weren't a spectator."

"No. You're right. I wasn't. I've improved. But still. I was only a passenger."

"What does that even mean? What's wrong with being a passenger?"

I kiss her on the forehead. It's more neutral. But it says: *Don't pull away*.

"I'm ready to be the driver. These guys are doing awful, awful things. Do I feel territorial about you? Of course. But what's happening is so egregious; it cannot be ignored. If we…no, if I do nothing, dozens of women will be trafficked this year. Sure, it's nothing compared to the tens of millions of humans trafficking globally. But it's something. And sometimes, something has to be enough."

•

If I had a dollar for every time I made a woman cry…I'd only have enough to buy a box of tissues—that's how hard I avoid it. OK, maybe a case of boxes of tissues.

•

We agree to tone it down for the night. Watch the movie. We start off on opposite sides of the couch. That lasts twenty minutes.

Tom Hardy's body on the screen makes me a bit insecure with my string-bean physique. By his third prison tour, Maya and I have been kissing for five minutes.

Another few minutes and she plants a knee, grabs my shoulders and straddles me. It's mechanical. It always feels tremendous to feel wanted. But this? It's like she's going through the motions. Doing all the right things. Maybe I'm too in my head. Maybe she'll say something goofy and original.

"Turn off the TV, baby."

•

She disrobes casually, as if she's alone, getting into the shower. I'm shocked by her confidence. And I'm also a little…I dunno…reluctant?

She grabs my hands. Puts them on her.

"Don't you want to touch me, baby?" *Baby* is such an advanced term to use. An established relationship term. It extends my hesitance.

She bulldozes through it.

She grabs me. Even over my jeans, the first glance of her hand on my penis feels like a mistake. But it's a mistake like ice cream at midnight. One I know I'm going to make.

Anticipation.

She unbuttons my pants and slides them off. I help a little, but I mostly watch. Her movements are natural, almost practiced.

With more hip flexibility than I believe possible, she leans, drops one foot, hip squats her tattered jeans down and off and then remounts me.

There's more.

She kisses me and leans back. Taking a long lick of her forefingers, she moistens the tip of my cock and pulls me straight into her. One motion.

Her being wet for me is a shallow way to feel validated, but I do.

Everything disappears except her moving ever so slightly on top of me and the sweet, sweaty smell of her neck.

·

8am.

I hear Frankie's footsteps coming toward us and grimace.

"Maya? You up? Wanna grab some tomatoes from the garden? I'll make some…"

Maya isn't up.

But I am.

"Ohhh."

I wave. Awkwardly. Trying not to wake Maya. I wish I'd worn a shirt to bed.

This was avoidable. Not a segue I would have chosen.

Frankie bites her lower lip and pulls her head from the doorway. I sneak out of bed, dress and follow.

Maya? Still dead asleep.

•

"Do you want me to grab those tomatoes from the garden?"

"Haven't you grabbed enough?"

•

Offering to drive downtown to buy coffee was the smartest thing I've done in twelve hours. We have coffee. I bought it. It's at home. Their home, not mine. Did Maya and I do something stupid? Yep. I can still smell her mixture of fruity potions on my t-shirt—from the hour we made out before taking our clothes off. Her lingering elixir is not effective negative reinforcement. It wasn't the best decision. I will not lie, sleeping in an actual bed over the van also wasn't terrible. Especially for certain things. Sex? Definitely. Going to the bathroom after? Absolutely.

I wake from my guilt-ridden daydream of nuzzling Maya's stomach and see that I'm already at the beach.

The two most natural things in Bolinas? Grabbing something from the garden and looking at the ocean.

Bolinas, CA—The Patch
Photo: A handful of guys at water's edge.
@georgeous Checking the surf = Bolinas TV.

•

Maya is awake. Seated across from Frankie. And they've both eaten. I see a plate for me. Fortunately, I brought three coffees back, instead of two.

I give Frankie hers first. An olive branch.

"Thanks. Your food may be cold by now." She looks pissed.

I hand Maya hers and slide the sugar towards her, across the kitchen island. I get the impression that I walked in on Frankie scolding Maya about the final scene in our movie-night last night.

"Yeah, I checked the surf and saw Team Brolinas about to paddle out."

"Assholes." Frankie takes a sip. "Well, I've gotta run. Deliveries. Thanks again for the coffee."

"'Course." I watch her grab her car keys and walk out the door. I feel like I'm in trouble. I turn to Maya.

"Hey."

"Hey."

"Am I in trouble?"

"Nooo...?"

"So yes."

"It's just..."

"Frankie?"

"Yeeah..."

"She's pissed?"

"Not exactly."

"Then what?"

"We just...sometimes. Sometimes we hook up."

"Hook up. Like make out? Kiss?"

"More."

"Whoa. Wow. So, she's not jealous of you, she's jealous of me."

She looks puzzled.

"Why would she be jealous of you?"

"Because of you. I thought she might be...I dunno...she's been flirty. Just a few times. But maybe I'm not reading it right." I repeat this last statement in my head. Idiotic. "Oh, god. That was so arrogant. I feel stupid."

"Not as stupid as the chick who just had eggies with the two people she sleeps with."

•

Maya is the hypotenuse of our love triangle. And she doesn't even know it. Actually, she probably doesn't care. How does she respond to the quizzical look on my face? She grabs our coffees and walks me to her bedroom.

•

She's fallen back asleep. What should I do? Select all that apply:

a) Let her sleep.
b) Wake her gently, by resting my manhood against her hip.
c) Take a photo for social media that I'd never post.
d) Finish her coffee.

Answer: c & d.

Bolinas, CA—The house
Photo: The cats dominating the bed.

@georgeous 3 cats. 2 people. 1 bed. @humanesociety

And no, not a single sliver of Maya's skin is visible. It's not that kind of photo. I'm not that kind of guy. The mental snapshots are more than enough.

•

Sitting in the van, drinking the last sugary drop of Maya's coffee, I try to be productive. Restless, again.

I wait another ten and then head back to the water. Liam had the same idea. My feelings for Maya contrast seeing Liam checking the tides so nonchalantly, after kicking the shit out of harmless Raj. My tenderness for Raj makes me realize that he really is my friend.

Seething, I head back.

•

I crack open the Mac.

Because I'm a near professional at overstaying my welcome, I moved the farm's router so that I can get WiFi more consistently in the van.

From: Lewis, George
To: Rogers, Timothy
Subject: More Life Skills

Hey Tim—

All is well here. I had a bit of a brainchild. Has Esquire ever done anything on maritime skills that are useful in everyday life? I feel like everyone wants to be Odysseus or Hemingway, but we're all land locked or life locked and never have a chance to learn things that would come in handy, like using a sailor's bowline knot to tie a Christmas tree to the top of a minivan.

Just a thought.

Let me know what you think.

Best,

George

\---

Still in draft, I rethink writing an email that's more straightforward:

Hey TR—

Can Esquire pay to teach me how to kill worthless, rapist, human traffickers?

Thanks,

G

I want to hit something. Instead, as usual, I hit delete.

I'd love to share more with TR. About my current predicament(s). Even to write a story about it. But I realize, accurately, that I am George Lewis—staff writer/amateur bro-skills columnist. Not George Lewis—crimefighter. Plus, highlighting my recent life experiences to a mass audience wouldn't do me any favors.

Instead, I pick up my phone.

"Sifu?"

"Yep! Hey George! How are you? And call me Mark!"

"Are you available for an extra session today? I feel like…"

"Of course! Come on in. I'm free noon 'til two."

"Perfect. I'm so glad you have a slot. I got kinda…"

"But don't be late! I'm going to dollar oyster happy hour. Beers are only three dollars. I don't want to miss it!" My visualization of him posting up at the Costco cheese sample table is not unfounded.

I wanted to chat with him. Just for a minute. To quell the anxiety.

I should not be craving a therapy session with the guy that teaches me how to hurt people.

•

"Wanna do some Judo? Wrestling moves? It's super fun!"

"OK?"

"It's fun! I promise!"

"Yeah, OK."

"You don't sound too enthusiastic!" Sifu Mark is fully bald, with a U-shaped fringe of dad hair. Blood moves visibility throughout his head when he's excited. And he's always excited.

"No. You're right. I have an agenda."

"Whatever you want, kiddo!"

"Remember when you said that first I had to learn how to kill someone, before I could hurt them?"

"It's true!"

"Can we go back to that?"

"How to kill? Of course! But George, why? Your magazine people told me to give you the variety pack. So you can write about it. Which is so, so exciting! You don't have to mention me, but I wouldn't mind it if you did! I'll sign a release. Is that what you call it?!" His eagerness is contagious. Even his terrible sweatpants make him look endearing.

"I'll pay for this one. Of course. And maybe a few extra?"

"And I'll charge you! Ha! But that's not what I mean." His brow furrows. "George. Do you feel unsafe?" He looks sad, like he just missed matinee pricing by three minutes. "What is it?"

"I just...I'm scared. There's some weird stuff going on. Things I don't have complete control of."

He marinates on my comment and then quickly snaps out of it.

"OK! Let's get you fixed up!"

•

"You look like Mr. Miyagi."

"I know, right?!"

Due to the proliferation of mixed martial arts, *The Karate Kid* umpire pads have been upgraded to a full contact kit. Rookie students, like yours truly, can learn to throw a real punch and gauge its impact.

He goes back through the motions from our first class. Forcing me to spar with him. Going faster. Driving me faster.

"Here's the thing, buddy. Faces make us mad. Sometimes so mad! We want to hit them and make the meanness stop."

"Agreed."

I think of Johnny's face.

"But that's short sided, kiddo. Look at my nose. A big one, right?!" I laugh. "But the sinuses were built to absorb blunt force impact. Think about it! Boogers cushion the blow!"

"Gross."

"You gotta hit'em where it hurts!"

In less than a second, he grazes my left eyeball, neck, chest, balls and toes. Jesus Christ, he is fast.

"Eyes. Throat. Solar Plexus. Groin. Feet. Even a great big monster will crumble, if you break one of the twenty bones in his feet!"

He goes again for my throat. But this time, I'm ready.

"Good! But you can't just react! You've gotta be defensive and offensive at the same time!"

"It's hard to do both at the same time. How do you do it so effortlessly?"

"It is hard! It takes practice!" If he does not coach soccer on the weekends, it is an enormous loss. *Time for orange slices, kiddos!*

I become entranced by blocking his movements and sprinkling in what he'd taught me in previous sessions.

"Throat. Feet. Throat. Solar Plexus. Feet. Eyeball. Throat. Groin. Groin. Feet." He barks at me, until I hit a rhythm. Until I can do it without thinking. "Good job buddy! Now, faster."

•

Sifu Mark has given me so much content; I don't know how to capture it for *Esquire*. Even though this was a personal class, a personal mission, it still seems relevant. And goddamn if he doesn't channel the wisdom of Bruce Lee, even in his own sneaking-candy-into-the-movie-theater kind of way. I'm at a loss as to how I can distill it into something thoughtful, cohesive. Something that might actually make it into the magazine. Even if it's only online.

Also, I'm starved.

Cannot remember being hungrier.

Again, parking drives every decision in San Francisco. Especially in the van. I'm a block from the Turkish guy I met a few days ago, but what I really want is to grab something quick. And after kung fu, maybe something Asian to eat? Racist? Possibly. Delicious? Probably.

There's no wind, and even though I'm shattered, I still have enough time to check the surf and maybe catch a few waves, if I can make it back to Bolinas by sunset.

•

"Georges?" The stylish counter guy at Common Sage pronounces it in an indistinct European accent. Not unlike my boy, Raj.

"Just plain old George. That's me. I know—no one has a 1950's name these days."

"Oh. No. You're right. Now I see that the 'S' is just a pen squiggle. You had two salmon omusubi and an Asian sandwich?"

"Yep. Did I over order?"

"Maybe. But didn't you just come from the gym?"

"Sort of. A kung fu hybrid class."

"Jeet Kune Do?"

"Yeah. How'd…"

"Then your meal choice is perfect!"

"But kung fu is Chinese. And you guys are Japanese fusion?"

"I'm a Bruce Lee fanatic. Obsessed." He pulls up his shirtsleeve, showing a massive *Enter the Dragon* tattoo. "You know he grew up just over the hill."

"I do."

"That's why your meal is perfect! A kung fu disciple destroying a Japanese enemy? Even food. It just seems…I dunno, so poetic. Sorry. Maybe it's too meta."

"Tremendous. Clearly you are the sage, here at Common Sage."

"Hardly." He rings up my bottle of soda water. "If only we could both be like water, I wouldn't have to overcharge you for Pellegrino."

10

The Groin. The expert's spot. After surfing every day, I feel like I'm ready.

I'm not.

It's big.

And I'm tired.

I paddle for one. Catch it. The bottom sucks out at the edge of the channel, grabs the rail of my board and slams me.

A dozen tumbles. I finally come up for air. Looking back outside, I see the bombs coming. Overhead. Maybe bigger. And I know I'm outmatched. I didn't ride a single wave. I catch the whitewater in on my belly, feeling like half a man. But that's not the half of it.

•

Out of the water, fully upright, feet firmly on the sand. It feels victorious. Safe.

Until I see them.

Johnny. Liam. Another dude, who looks as stupid as he is pretty.

They're waiting.

For me.

•

Bolinas, CA—The Groin

Photo: My van. The sunset. The ocean. Three bros.

@georgeous If one guy is watching your car? He's a valet. Two guys? The valet shift change. Three guys? That's a gang.

"Professor! Didn't see you catch one! You sick?"

Nothing is more condescending than an insincere nickname. I, too, am no stranger to this weapon.

"I'm just learning. You know. Kinda like you with running a business. And, uh, Liam with English as his second language."

I know I'm done. I may as well enjoy it.

I look at the third guy. A pretty boy. He's licking his lips, waiting for the green light from Johnny.

"Idn't time you mosey on back to LA?"

"True. Soon. Why? You wanna carpool?"

Johnny grits his teeth. But not that hard. He knows that he's already won.

I size him up. Throat. Groin. Feet.

I've got one shot. I could disable Johnny. He wouldn't anticipate me striking first. But I don't have the game to hit him decisively and then take out the other two guys. Even though part of me thinks I'm pretty fucking ninja, after five hours of training.

But damn.

I'm so, so tired.

My only card? Make the beating swift.

"The Long Beach Harbor can handle those big Maersk ships, no problem. Think of how many women you could traffic!"

Bam.

From behind, Pretty Boy hits me in the back of the head. Not that hard. Like a gift. Like it's not my fault. The torrent of blows are swift. I take solace in knowing it won't be long. And knowing my payback plan is already underway.

A phone rings.

"*Teenage. Mutant. Ninja. Turtles...*" Even while being beaten, I have to give props for this ringtone.

The fetal position.

Kick. Punch. Kick. Punch.

"Hello? Bri-guy, what's up?" Liam thinks this is as good a time to take a call. From the direction of his voice, I know the last kick I feel is his.

And then?

They just walk away.

A pretty half-assed beat down, if you ask me.

•

Pain. But not as much as I'd expected. More of a message than a true beating.

I turn my head, to check that my sanctuary of the van is still there.

It is. With a rock jutting out of its now flat tire.

•

"Oh my god. What the fuck?"

My face has seen better days. And the rest of me is covered in spare tire filth.

"Ice. Please."

•

Sometimes a shower makes you feel like a new man. Sometimes it makes you feel wet and broken.

The latter.

•

Maya.

We talk.

I hurt.

Then I deflect.

I hurt. But I still pacify.

But not that hard.

She takes her turn.

Ice. Tenderness. Soft touching.

She grabs my dick.

"Maya, I can't."

She looks deflated.

Almost more than me.

Almost.

•

I need to write my mom a postcard. She loves knowing what I'm doing. No matter how mundane, trivial or brutally honest:

Mom—Car broke down. Stuck for a few days. Safe. Don't worry. —G

Mom—Fun night. Hungover. Nursing it with a swim. Maybe a coconut water. Then maybe coconut water & vodka ;). —G

She repeats, time and time again, "Just tell me. Tell me anything. I just want to know what you're up to. I promise. I won't get offended. I won't judge." I am candid with her. And offering that vulnerability has made us much closer over the years. It also helps me stay grounded. Keeps me in check. Keeps me thinking: *What would mom say, if I sent her a postcard of what I'm doing right now?*

And then there's this.

That current postcard would illustrate me cuddling with my bedmate—that is unlikely to be my future bride—and nursing a bloody nose.

•

Morning.

Stiffness.

Maya's gone.

The wind tells me that the surf is blown. It doesn't matter. I don't have the motivation to squeeze my body into a wetsuit, anyway.

•

Brothers in arms, I swing by The Bookstore. Raj is there. This makes me smile.

Plus, he is such a gangster.

Is he shying away from his daily routine, from intimidation?

Nope.

Is he wearing makeup, maybe foundation?

Yep.

This exchange in my brain gives me hip hop lyric déjà vu, but I can't place it.

"Monsieur Georges."

"Mon ami."

"Ce qui est arrivé à votre visage."

"I'm guessing, 'Wow, your face looks fucked up.'?"

"Oui."

"Same as you. I have until yesterday to leave Bolinas. Fuck those guys."

He shakes his head. Disgusted. Both by Team Brolinas and my tasteless swearing.

"Raj?"

"Oui."

"What does your name mean? Is it Hindi? Sorry, I know there are hundreds of languages and dialects."

He blushes, and it penetrates the thick layer of foundation.

"Raj is my middle name. It was my father's name. My true first name is Ajit. It's Sanskrit. It means unbeatable."

•

A chat. Shared empathy. Our first hug. It's gentle. We both wince. I wonder if The Bookstore has a homeopathic medicine section.

"Monsieur Georges, come with me. I need you to meet someone."

"But who will watch the shop?" I smirk.

Monsieur Raj is wearing a banker's collared shirt, with a tasteful herringbone sweater. I didn't quite expect him to walk me into 2 Mile Surf Shop.

"Blake."

"Raj! What's up, my brotha!"

Blake is owning a moustache that is simultaneously ironic and natural. It works. Drill in hand, he's installing an eight foot tall great white shark jaw on an empty wall.

"This is George." He drops the French pronunciation. Raj is so cute.

"Hey man!"

Blake sets the drill on top of the footstool and gives me a firm handshake. Like he's been expecting me. He looks an extra second at my face, then over at Raj's. He should see my back.

"Let's cruise over to the shaper's room."

"But who'll watch the shop?" This time, I actually mean it.

Raj leans into my ear.

"Blake is more of an artist in residence. He doesn't sell surfboard wax."

"I wasn't suggesting that."

Blake hits the shaping room and, hearing voices, turns back around.

"Let's go back to the wetsuit rental shack. It's a better spot, anyway. Have you seen my totems?"

Blake turns broken surfboards into art. A modern day Renaissance man, with recycled materials and ancient influence. Hence the moustache.

"Very cool. Original. And kinda timeless, given the medium."

"Thanks, homie."

We take them in. One is a giant pelican. Its beak is intricately painted with a majestic seascape. $450. I'm tempted to buy it. With tax, it'd wipe out the entirety of my 401(k). Plus, it's way too big for the living room of the van.

"You're with Frankie, right? Sleeping over?"

Uh oh.

"Uhhh, yeah? I've been crashing there. In my van." Hearing myself say this out loud, I hear how suspect it is.

"Naw, naw. Yeah, I just meant staying there. I know you've been hooking up with Maya."

"Jesus."

"Sorry, bro. Small town. We only have one bar."

"Right."

"The only time I can catch up with Frankie is at Smiley's. Otherwise, I'd have seen you at the farm by now. But that's currently a no-fly zone."

I look puzzled. Raj leans in, again.

"They used to be an item. Blake and Frankie."

"You were her boyfriend?"

"Yeah."

"I thought she liked…"

"Girls? Ha! No. She's just a strong woman. And open. Really open."

"That makes sense." It kinda does. I still have no idea why Raj brought me here.

"Frankie told me. About your rough plan. The fuel lines. Boom boom."

"What? Are there any secrets in this town?"

"Not really. But don't worry. It's just us. And we'd all be in such great jeopardy to have it get out, no one will say a word."

I hope he's right.

"Sorry. I'm at a complete loss. Why…?"

"I'm engaged. My fiancé is crazy jealous. So, I've gotta steer clear of Frankie. But I still care about her. Plus, I fucking hate those guys. Hate them."

"OK?"

"The enemy of my enemy is my friend." He points to me. I've always loved this quote.

"OK?"

"The boat. The plan."

Blank stare.

"Uhhh…"

"You're gonna need a boat. One that's not out of place. One from here."

"OK?"

His impatience with my lack of understanding jacks up his intensity.

"I have a boat! I can help! I want to help!"

"Ohhh. Gotcha. Sorry."

"And I need to do it through you. Or my lady will have my ass."

"She knows?"

"No way. And, other than ordering a draft at the bar, I can't be seen with Frankie. People talk."

"So I hear."

"The wedding is only a month away. I want to keep the water calm."

Raj brightens.

"You two will have such beautiful children!"

"Ha. Thanks. If they look like her."

I gaze at his other art pieces and try to work this thing out. Blake picks it back up.

"Half of this town is either intimidated by these clowns or paid off by them."

I turn to Raj.

"Like the Mexican drug cartels. Plata o plomo?" Raj questions my Spanish. "Silver" I hold out my hand to take a bribe, "or lead." I pantomime a gun shooting a bullet. "Nothing in between."

Blake shakes his head, with something to add.

"But there's another faction here. The silent majority. They're not being bribed nor threatened. Them? They just want them gone. Not just gone. Because no one ever fully leaves Bolinas. Ideally? They want them to disappear." We all shrug in agreement.

"You guys are OK with me leading the charge? It has been pointed out to me, several times, that I don't even live here."

"That's exactly why."

Raj turns to me, with the first serious face I've ever seen on him.

"And, because no one was getting beat up, until you got here."

Bolinas, CA—2 Mile Surf Shop
Photo: Seven broken surfboards, assembled and painted into a single bird beast.
@georgeous Totally bizarre, totemly awesome. @totemsandfloatems

•

Blake isn't just a boat owner, he's a true seaman. He also emphasized the intangibility of maritime law. How Johnny and crew were abusing it and how we could use it to our advantage. Google seconds his opinion:

Murder Case Stalled for Years—Maritime Law Unenforceable

Maritime Law—A Law or a Loophole?

Car or Boat? Traffickers take to the High Seas to Avoid Prosecution

•

There's something about premeditation that catalyzes anxiety.

Afraid you're gonna die? Knock out the simplest task you can complete. To feel grounded. To feel progress. To feel normal.

From: Lewis, George
To: Rogers, Timothy
Subject: Bruce #4

Tim—

Continued progress below. Again, very much appreciated your guidance on simply writing (semi) polished notes versus complete pieces. For some reason, that slightly lowered bar has removed a lot of angst. Thank you.

Best,

George

Bruce Lee #4

I'm 6'3 now, but I wasn't always. I was small. And I've experienced senseless aggression many, many times. Schoolyard fights, sure. But the smaller things are what break you. When I was a freshman swimmer in high school, we used to go to 7-Eleven before practice. One time, I walked outside with my Slurpee. A varsity guy grabbed it, took a sip and poured the rest on the ground. Just because he could. Knowing I'd do nothing.

I'd like to think that I'm a borderline pacifist, yet violence occupies my mind every day. Maybe not as often as love but definitely more often than planning for the future. Why? Because even in my self-directed adult life, I experience constant reminders. A sketchy guy enjoying too long of a glance at my girl, while we're at the movies. And letting it linger. Because he can. How many times has this happened to me? Hundreds? Thousands? It feels like more.

These nameless adversaries are who occupy my tense daydreams and whom I fight in my nightmares. Prompting me to shadow box, while waiting for the shower water to get warm.

But actually taking a swing and connecting? To another human body? It's scary and exhilarating and fulfilling. Because I've been waiting forever to do it. To do it correctly. To truly stand tall.

But then? The fantasy ends. The dread returns. When? The moment I miss. The moment all of my fury and being bullied and picked on ends in a fistful of air.

Swing. Swing. Swing. Hit. Hit. Miss. That one miss tells me that maybe I should have stayed out of the ring. Because ignoring my fears may be weak. But facing my fears may be deadly.

11

Frankie greets me, as I pull into my makeshift campsite—a short, wide path off the driveway.

"You look fuuucked up. What does she look like?"

"You are fucked up."

She giggles. I've never met anyone like Frankie who relishes being called out. Correction: I've met many. But the others couldn't pull it off. Not without some latent resentment.

"Are you OK?"

"I'm fine. It's not too, too bad."

"Need I ask?"

"Nope."

She scrunches her face in pure empathy. She reaches out to touch me but stops short. Not sure where the bruises might be. This makes her face sad. It makes me sad, too. Because she's so much more in tune with other people's needs than most. Including Maya. A thought to overanalyze at another time.

"So, Blake?"

"Yup. How was the meet?"

"What's the longest something can stay private in this town?"

"I fucked him. The night before his engagement. That's a secret. Did he tell you that?"

"Nope."

"See. Some people can keep a secret. And you. You keep that one to yourself."

"Jesus, Frankie."

"I thought they were gonna break up. I swear."

I shake my head.

"Why did you tell me that? I didn't need to know that."

"So you know we're in this together. So you can trust me. You can, you know."

"I know. I already do."

"Good, 'cause I deserve it. I'm honest. And you've got a little thing for me. But you won't admit it." My jaw drops. "Don't act surprised, George. Clearly we both have the same taste in women."

"Wow. You're really liking yourself right now. Admittedly, you should." I pull beers from the cooler. She opens hers off the door brace of the van, with a slap of her palm. Fierce. Takes a swallow.

"Still cold. When did you last replace the ice?"

"Five days ago. The Yeti. It's legit."

"Cheers to that."

We look out over the farm. A few minutes pass. Farm time.

"Blake is such a sweetheart. Super talented but still down to earth. His lady would be devastated, if she found out about you two."

"Blake? I was in love with him. I thought there was still some semblance of a chance. I'd still stand barefoot on burning coals, just to sit across the table and drink lukewarm tea with him."

"Wow."

"Fuck you!"

"No, no. That's so sweet. It's the nicest thing I've ever heard you say. About anyone. It's humbling."

Another pregnant pause.

"You guys are kinda similar. In some ways. Both driven. But not in a mainstream way." This? I was not expecting.

"Thank you. Geez. You're such a lover today."

"Fuck you."

"And she's back. OK. So Blake. He can help?"

"Yeah. He doesn't just have a boat; he has skills. He's constantly taking it out, searching for driftwood, tsunami wreckage—stuff he can turn into art. He knows this coastline like the back of his hand." Her face gets somber.

"He seems rock solid. But it's such a big risk. He's so down. It's almost like he's going to bat, I dunno, a little too hard?"

"So what?"

I don't back down.

"Your ex-boyfriend, who's about to get married to someone that's insanely jealous of you, is willing to commit a pretty serious crime. For you. It seems messy."

"You may know everyone in this town, but you don't know everything, George."

"Jesus. Frankie, I'm not the enemy. You do know that, right?"

"Sorry. I…Did Maya tell you? Where she came from?"

"Yeah, Phoenix."

"And what her job was there?"

"She was a hostess or something?"

"Or something."

"What?"

"That's not my secret to share."

"At this point, we have no secrets."

"That's not true, and you know it."

"We have no secrets that, if not shared, jeopardize our current mission. To stop some bad guys. If it's relevant, please tell me."

"Ugh. I hate this."

"Frankie, we have to trust each other. And I can keep a secret."

"I'm sure you can." She says it both sarcastically and as a compliment. She pauses. Thinks. "OK. OK. She was a prostitute."

"What?"

"Yeah."

"I don't…"

"Believe it. She had a fucked up childhood. Fucked. Up. Her uncle thought she was his side-girl. Started when she was eleven."

"Oh my god."

"Ran away at seventeen. No education. No job prospects."

"Ugh."

"So, she throws on some makeup to look twenty-two. Becomes the go to party girl at some fancy hotel. Not too bad. Only has to fuck one traveling businessman a week. She even saved a little money. A decent gig for a few years. I mean, look how beautiful she is."

"Yeah, but that is awful. Beyond awful."

"Wait for it. A few more years pass. Then some local thugs notice her hustle. See her as a lucrative revenue stream. They still keep her high end. But then it's not once a week, it's once a day."

The most painful part of this story? How believable it is. She continues.

"By the time she gets to Bolinas, she's a wreck."

"And that makes her jump straight into Johnny's arms? From the frying pan to the fire. Ooof."

"Well, it was Johnny 1.0. He used to be less douchey. More charming. Still a prick but more tolerable."

I shake my head and return to listening.

"They date for a while. She's in heaven. So in love. I get her a job at the bar. Everything's perfect. She even goes for an STD test and only has a little treatable case of chlamydia."

"Frankie!"

"Oh, like you weren't thinking it."

"Fair. Fuuuck. And I'm guessing this story doesn't end up with Johnny on a white horse?"

"Nope. Johnny has a bad history of owing money."

"Of course he does."

"Maya wants to help. 'What can I do?' But she only knows how to pull beers and pull…"

"Don't."

"So, she blows a guy. Gets Johnny off the hook for some $300 broken motorcycle purchase."

"He cuts his teeth on her."

"Exactly."

"How'd she get out?"

"I got her to transfer her co-dependence to me."

I cringe at her word choice.

"Better than the alternative, I guess. And Johnny just let her go?"

"Not entirely. But he took off for a pot-trimming gig up in Humboldt."

"He was a trimmigrant?"

"Surprised?"

"Nope. Zero. I just love that term. I could say it every day."

"You're hardly a mystery, George. A clean, dry wetsuit and a penchant for portmanteaus."

"That's a great word, too. Underutilized. Although I can never pronounce it correctly."

She shakes her head at the interruption.

"So, Johnny's gone for half a year or more. Makes some connections up north for his current, eh, entrepreneurial endeavor. It kept him busy. He comes back and doesn't suck Maya back in. But he doesn't let her go entirely, either. Not 100%." She looks me hard in the eyes. "George, you can't think your face looks like that just because you picked the wrong town to surf in."

•

"Does Maya hook up with you because...

"As payment for me taking care of her? You asshole!"

"No! I meant...I dunno...to feel safe?"

"We hook up because it feels good. Plus, it's cold in Bobo at night, with no central heat."

•

From: Rogers, Timothy
To: Lewis, George
Subject: Checking in on you

George—

I'm not one to pry, and I am enjoying your pieces. The philosophy of violence and fear? A grand departure from your cheeky, funeral sex Tweets but a welcome one.

I did want to check in with you, personally. George, you're a Staff Writer for Esquire. Esquire prides itself on true immersion journalism, and that's becoming your sweet spot, possibly to a fault. Your pieces are a bit intense and appear to be getting more so. Please try not to over-immerse yourself, OK?

Best,

TR

Ugh. TR. Bad timing.

So tired. I need to get a huge night's sleep.

I walk into the house. Frankie's waiting for a webpage to load from the molasses-slow internet.

"Mind if I shower?"

"'Course. You know you don't need to ask."

"I know. But I do. If not for you, for me. I don't live here. Shouldn't forget that."

"Okaaay…" She's barely listening.

"Sorry, I'm in a weird mood."

"Welcome to Bobo." Her screen bursts with light. "Yes!" Facebook fully loads. The next half an hour? Adios. She doesn't even notice me walk away.

Standing in front of the mirror, I take my clothes off and assess the damage. Overnight, the smaller bruises on my back have expanded. They've gone from black to purple, and a few of them now connect. I look like a grape-flavored Holstein cow.

Knock, knock.

"Yeah, come in." I don't know who it is. But it doesn't matter. None of us has anything left to hide.

Maya, cold beer first, pops her head in.

"Oh my god." She takes in the awful sight of me. "I wanted to bring you one for the shower."

I grab it.

"Perfect. Thank you."

She let's go of the door handle and lets gravity sweep it fully open.

"I didn't realize you'd be nude, checking yourself out in the mirror. You know, like a girl."

"Neither did I." I look straight into the mirror and flex my puny right bicep. But I can only hold it for a second. She laughs. It's a small exchange, but I needed to hear it. Her happy. If only for a second. I don't have the energy to tackle what I learned today.

She presses on a bruise on my shoulder blade, lightly.

"Ouch."

"Sorry! You look terrible."

I take a swig of the beer, reach into the shower and set the bottle in the corner soap tray, stepping in after.

"I know."

•

My pajamas are clean. A threadbare t-shirt and some light cotton pants that never acted as actual pants. Well, not for me. They'd be formalwear at a music festival. It's all I can do to stand on one leg at a time and get them on. They smell amazing. Whenever I relish clean smells, I know I'm sleepy.

I walk out to my roommates. They're engrossed in talking, as always. Their computers and phones next to them look lonely, wishing to be loved by other, more attentive millennials.

"Mind if I grab a beer? I'm cooked. Gonna go to bed."

"Yeah, us too."

I pull a beer, open it and walk down the hallway. My van seems like it's a million miles away. And enticing, too. I reach Maya's room but don't look in. It seems like such a hassle to even attempt to get an invite. I don't have the stamina to spoon, let alone offer anything else.

I can hear Maya's soft footsteps behind me.

"George. My room. Don't go to the van."

•

I sit at the edge of the bed. On what has become my de facto side. Romantic habits manifest so quickly.

Maya comes in, acting her sweetest. She pets me, softly.

"Hey, would it be OK if Frankie sleeps with us?"

"Like *The Three Little Bears?*"

"Yeah. Without the creepy shared DNA."

"Why don't I just go to my van? Seriously, I don't care. You guys can do whatever you want."

"But we want you here."

I sigh, because that's the exact answer I wanted to hear. I pick the beer up. Take a sip.

"I'm not mad or hurt. I am the guest here. There is so much going on. It's insane. I'm happy to have some downtime. I don't need to be your new instant boyfriend, just add water."

"Boyfriend!"

"You want that?"

"No!"

"I didn't think so. Maya, I'm sorry. I'm so spent. I honestly don't know what we're talking about. I like you guys. Care about you guys. And we sort of have a mission, even if the circumstances are awful.

That's it. It's that simple."

"I know."

"We both do." I didn't even see Frankie walk in. "Just get in bed, George."

12

I'm skinny but tall. So, not small. Maya and Frankie are both short-ish but fit. Even a king-sized bed isn't big enough for my two wildflower queens and their third-wheel companion.

Have I ever thought about this moment? Fantasized about it? Yes, but not like this. In my fantasy, I'm in the middle, and they're fighting over me. In this version? I'm on the side, dozing, while they nestle forever to get comfortable. Forever. Maya is diplomatically in the middle. Of course.

I look at my watch. 9pm—aka Farm Midnight.

•

Actual midnight.

Psychosomatically, I wake to licking my lips. They are dry, but it's the sound that wakes me up. The sound of the two of them kissing makes me crave Burt's Bees lip balm.

Smack, smack, smack.

Even the sound highlights that they both prefer the long, lingering kisses. Who doesn't.

I get up to go pee. They pause their make out sesh but just for a second.

The mirror greets me. I look terrible. Van or cramped bed of two lovers? Now that I'm pseudo awake, I can at least go back and grab my warm beer. I wash my hands and, for good measure, thoroughly cleanse my man-parts with moist wipes so they're minty fresh. You never know.

I've been gone three minutes, and their bed posture has changed. They're not going at it, knocking it out. They're snug. Covers up. Both with their backs touching each other. Looking cozy in the NorCal night air. Both watch me, following my movements in the room.

Maya reaches across my third of the bed and steals a sip of my beer.

"You look tired."

"I am. Also, never say that phrase to anyone, under any circumstances."

Frankie looks like she feels guilty. Or wants me to leave. Or both.

"Do you want us to stop?"

"Nope. This was happening way before I got here. Do you want me to go? Seriously. I so don't care if…"

"Please, no. Stay."

"Yeah, stay." Frankie seconds her.

I crawl into bed.

Like the second day after lifting weights, I feel worse, more sore. Every bruise feels agitated, pulsing with trapped blood.

"Ooof."

"You alright?" Frankie asks, with legitimate concern.

"We need to get those motherfuckers."

"Yeah. Somethin'. But not tonight. Let's just enjoy tonight."

"I don't know that I have it in me. And there're so many weird layers, I ..."

Maya kisses me.

"Stop thinking. Just be here. Just be here, with us."

•

They kiss and fondle for so long, I almost fall back asleep. Maya throws me a few obligatory chest strokes, but they fade. Especially when Frankie fully commits to devouring Maya's lady-parts.

Frankie has skills.

Maya starts to go. It's not gonna be a huge one, but Frankie sure served this appetizer up quick. Maya reaches to her left. Grabs my arm. She digs her nails into me, and it hurts. But in a good way. She finishes. I'm ecstatic, because all I want to do is sleep.

They do some groping. I hope Frankie is equally quick. Let's face it—passive threesomes are a hassle. What's worse? Passive aggressive threesomes—aka me letting this one happen to me and acting like I'm not totally into it. Because that's just not true. I'm elated to even be invited.

I let go. I close my eyes and search for the pillow's firmest spot. Found it.

The deep blackness and slight decent that defines *falling asleep*? I'm there.

Frankie orgasms in a quiet, efficient burst. Pragmatic, even in ecstasy.

It's a wrap. I drop instantly into a blissful slumber.

An indeterminate amount of time passes. A minute? An hour? The pain has me dreamless. I wake to a sprinkle of sugar on my lips.

Kiss, kiss.

"You asleep?"

I kiss Maya back. A little lazily but more than I thought I had in me.

"Yep."

Maya nuzzles my neck. Frankie and I have kept our distance all night. Respectful of boundaries and our shared lover. Until now. Now, I realize that the finger tickling the side of my shoulder is Frankie. Her touch is so soft. Subtle. Tickle, tickle, stroke. A touch that is 100% for the other person.

I don't think that Maya is an inherently selfish person. Followers are pleasers, always leaning toward selfless. It's something I, too, struggle with. But she is an opportunist. And I know she's not done coming. So, when she takes me in her mouth, I know that it's not all for me.

My hands haven't even grazed Frankie this whole time. Not even accidentally. I plan to keep it that way. Unless she volunteers.

Every inch of my body aches. I've both given up and am trying to stay hard at the same time. I refocus on staying hard.

The fucking cats. They see the full bed and wander around curiously. Circumnavigating our entangled bodies, they distract me from my current goal. Maya's in a rhythm, and she can witness the results. The blood flows from my endless bruises into my member. I feel the re-stiffening, and I'm almost impressed with myself. Almost. Frankie adds a cherry on top, by rolling her hands across my torso.

The moment the cats exit, Frankie sits up on her heels. Tall. Half strong. Half erotic. She keeps one hand stroking my shoulder. The other hand?

She waits. Waits until we lock eyes. Slides the backside of her hand across her cheek. Lets her fingernails linger on her neck. Strokes the gulf in between her breasts. Down.

Back.

Again.

She's not so much stroking herself as she is showing herself. To me. Sharing herself with me. Inviting me to see her.

Maya notices. Not us. Not Frankie and me. She notices that I'm rock hard.

She stops. Abruptly. Half smiles. In a single swift motion, she straddles me. Pulls me inside of her. Just like the first time. On the couch. Sexual muscle memory is bionic.

The moment of penetration is bittersweet. I, too, feel like an opportunist, receiving pleasure from someone that's experienced so much trauma. But I realize that all three of us are opportunists. And all three of us feel good right now.

The second (and probably last) pseudo threesome of my life. It's just as weird and unimaginable as the first. The word *threesome* sounds tantalizing, but in my experience, it's just a pseudonym for: *awkward while naked.*

My two girls. Sharing themselves with me. It's sacred.

Maya is getting after it. Self-absorbed. Frankie slides an open palm a few inches closer to me. Daring me to take it.

I do.

For ten seconds, I stroke her hand. Each finger, individually. Like a singular task. Then I take her hand and cup it underneath Maya's left breast. So Maya can feel Frankie's contact—and also my force behind it.

That's all Maya needed. The connection. The absence of judgment.

She goes. She's worked for it. And it's big. She collapses on top of me. I'm glad I could make her come. That we could make her come. I'm equally glad Frankie didn't let go of my hand.

Phew. Well done by all. Time for sleep. I shift my hips, proposing a Maya dismount.

Nope.

Her knees grip my battered torso. A bit too hard.

"Ow!"

"Sorry! I thought you liked it close!"

Frankie finds this shared intimacy hilarious and breaks.

"Keep it close, George!"

"I hate you guys."

Maya giggles. With me inside her. It feels fantastic.

She laughs a last time, then puts her hips back to work.

"Can you come, baby? I want you to come." It's her go to. Calling me *baby*. It still sounds rehearsed. And, like last time, she says it with her eyes closed. I'm not sure why. Maybe it's detachment? But no matter what, she's trying. Trying to be sweet. And I can at least try, too.

It's an odd sensation to keep reminding yourself to be appreciative during a threesome. But, let's face it, being tormented is my bit.

Frankie grips my hand, again. She presses it against Maya's chest. Elsewhere. Forceful and strong. But sensual. I'm actually learning a lot tonight.

"Just try, George. It's OK if you can't. But just try. We want you to feel good."

So do I.

Maya's knees go back to: *Just how you like it.* I do. With Maya on top of me, they start kissing and fondling, again.

Still holding Frankie's hand, I subtly coax her back. Back to me. Maya is pumping me and Frankie exits their kiss with a long hard drag along Maya's chest and thigh. Maya whisper-squeals. It sounds like she's got another one in her.

Frankie pins my forehead down with her hand. Like she can read my mind.

Understood.

She drags her right nipple against my left eye. Continuing along my nose and lower cheek.

Then she kisses me.

Actually, she bites me. Our first kiss is a bite. It's soft. But it reveals her hunger.

I look up at Maya. Stroke up over her tits and then back down. She rides me like it's a task. One that must be completed. Then? She looks at Frankie kissing my neck, then back at me. She gives me a knowing glance. It says: *It's OK. Let Frankie do her thing. And it's OK if you're into it. Just let go.*

At least that's what I hear in my mind.

I keep my hands to myself, letting the two of them control the balance.

But Frankie has her own agenda.

She grabs the back of my head with her left hand. Presses her right hand firmly on my left pec. On my heart.

Then?

Then she kisses me, like it's the last thing she'll ever do.

Whatever she does, it works.

•

7am.

I've had dreams about someone I used to think was insignificant or innocuous. Someone I had one hundred percent compartmentalized. It's even happened while awake, daydreaming. Today, it's the first thing I think of, when I quietly get out of bed.

Even though I'm fully rested, I'm still in a haze. Frankie. My compartmentalization of her is gone. It's been replaced by something more certain and even more uncertain. Maya? I know even less about her now than the day I met her.

But I can't stop thinking about Frankie. I've seen a warmth in her that I can't remember ever experiencing. Other than it feeling familiar.

Hopeful.

The things we crave, even if unknown, always feel like memories, once experienced. No wonder we crave so many things.

Leaving the room, I turn and look at my bedmates. They share the bed in a symbiotic way. Not spooning but still connected.

I leave them in good hands. Each other's. And craving two things: coffee and a surf.

•

Bolinas, CA—Coast Cafe
Photo: Empty paper coffee cup, with Gorge misspelled in Sharpie.
@georgeous Who doesn't know how to spell George (Washington!)?

"Professor. Surprised to still see you here."

Fuck.

It's just after 7:30am. I thought I was safe. I thought I had time. I thought I could sneak in, before being noticed.

The sheriff's car parked out front calmed me even further. Mistake. The moment I see Johnny, I bow my head. Subservient. Like his bitch. Because, locking eyes with him as I near the door, I can see that's what he expects. Even grabbing a coffee in Bolinas—he's the gatekeeper. He leans against the wall, impeding my entry.

"Three more days and I'm gone. I swear. Just three more."

"Three? Sounds like a lot more than zero."

"I just need a few more days to finish my piece. That's it. I swear. Please, man."

Johnny is so hungry for dominance, he eats it up. He's pleased that

I have to grovel. And that the bruise on my cheek is still visible. He can't hear me gritting my teeth. He can't sense me wanting to punch him in the throat.

He keeps savoring his triumph. Like a sip of fine wine. Me being supplicant must taste delicious. My weakness. Forced into a corner.

He smiles, sucking his alpha dog-ness into his chest. Smug. He owns me, as we stand in front of the cops. Both of us with separate, silent agendas.

Liam bursts through the front door, the wily little sycophant.

"Gentlemen! One light, one sweet. Here you go!" Liam hands the coffees through the passenger-side window.

Johnny nods at the cops and doesn't even pretend to downplay his overt intimidation of me. If anything, he flaunts it. Thanks a lot, Marin County Sheriff's Department.

"Thank you for your service!" Liam's robotic singsong of the phrase makes him sound like a psychopath. Accurate.

Liam has tucked several hundred-dollar bills in between their coffee cups and their cardboard sleeves.

I should have made coffee at home.

Liam walks toward us, drinking his coffee thirstily. Like he's thirsty for another swing. My body cringes.

The cops drive away. Liam salutes them, awkwardly. The only way he knows how to do anything. Johnny smiles. Almost condescendingly. Like watching misbehaving interns leave the office of the VP.

I've still not walked inside to order.

"Three days, Professor. Not four. Yah heard?"

His *Mississippi Burning* drawl is back.

"I heard."

Fucking idiot. I only need two days. Because his rendezvous with his female cargo out at sea is the day after tomorrow. In three days, he isn't gonna want to bully me. He's gonna want to kill me.

•

"Hey."

"Hey!"

"Here."

"Thanks!" The three coffee ritual returns. Frankie is awake, rummaging through the kitchen. Maya is still asleep.

Before I stupidly ask: *Are we cool?*, she grabs her coffee and sweeps a hand down my chest. Sweetly suggesting: *Yeah, we're cool.*

I can't help myself.

"You're an incredible kisser."

"I know." She giggles. "You have nice hands. But you keep them to yourself too much."

"I was trying to be…"

"I know, George. No fucking duh. I appreciate it."

I lean over and kiss her on the forehead. She kisses me back on the lips.

"This is gonna get so fucking weird."

"Isn't it already?"

"Ha."

"Just enjoy it until it gets fucked up. Can you do that? I doubt it. But let's at least try. OK?"

"Well spoken." I kiss her. A little more. Set my hands on her.

The toilet flushes. Maya. I'm pretty sure she'll go back to bed, but I still feel like we're gonna get caught. Be in trouble.

Frankie doesn't care.

We kiss. And kiss. Like high schoolers.

I've had sex with Maya a few times now. But this PG-13 kitchen rendezvous with Frankie feels more intimate.

She can feel me stiffen and doesn't shy away from it. She takes my hands. Guides them. Neck. Chest. Ass.

Again.

It oddly reminds me of kung fu training, and takes me out of my trance, but I let it go.

I kiss her and smile.

"Why do women love hands so much?"

"Good hands. We love good hands."

"Seems odd. Out of all of the body parts. You know?"

"You look at a guy's hands. Wondering what they'll feel like when they're on you. So how they look is important. It's part of the fantasy."

•

We've moved on to homemade coffee and ginger tea. I don't drink tea. Tea is for sick people.

We've finally stopped making out and have been talking about nothing and everything for over an hour. Maybe two.

Maya walks out sleepily, and Frankie is wearing my weather-worn, soft-as-silk hoodie and stretching it out with her knees pulled up inside. Such disregard for my coveted items is strictly forbidden. But, after seeing my two best friends naked simultaneously, even I have to loosen up a bit.

The moment I find peace, she reaches for her tea, yanks the sleeve up to her elbow and decimates the wrist elastic.

I'm not sure if Maya will be territorial about me and/or my hoodie, but I expect something.

She takes in the scene.

Nothing.

Not threatened. Not mad.

Nothing.

She looks relieved. Just for a second, it looks like a weight has been lifted from her shoulders. As if she was anticipating a relationship talk she really didn't want to have.

"Morning!"

"We split your coffee, sleepyhead." Frankie covers for me.

"That's not true. I drank it." I try to maintain some sense of manhood. I don't know why.

"No worries. Kinda craving tea anyway. Water still hot?"

"Should be."

That's it? The conclusion to last night is: *Who wants a cup of Darjeeling?*

•

It's been a long, slow morning. But the anxiety is slowly resurfacing. I remain perplexed at how we'll pull this off. Foiling Team Brolinas. How we'll even pull off having the meeting to plan how we might pull this off.

None of us has showered. We're all spattered with love juice, underneath comfy clothes. I want to coax them back into bed. But I want to discuss black ops logistics even more. When it comes to getting things done, there's only one person to talk to: Frankie.

"To meet up, would you guys be open to us using Smiley's? Maybe the office upstairs? Late night, after closing?"

"No fucking way. Too many after-hours drug deals in the parking lot. We need somewhere equally central that's more innocuous."

Maya, passive as a wallflower, is even quieter than normal. When she pipes up, it's pronounced.

"I'm all for saving the girls. For sure. But isn't there a pretty good chance someone's gonna get hurt? Badly hurt?"

"It's not off the table." I say it without thinking.

Frankie does not respond as calmly.

"Would that be the worst thing? Fuck those guys. Maya look! Look at George's face! You know, the guy that grocery shops for us and that you fucked last night?"

"I know. I know. It just seems a little extreme, yah know?"

"Are you serious? They traffic twenty-year-old girls from tiny Siberian hamlets? And you're worried that Johnny might scrape his elbow?"

Maya answers, only able to make eye contact with her tea.

"They're not such bad guys. That stuff happens everywhere. They're just trying to get by. There aren't a lot of opportunities in Bolinas."

Frankie looks like she might hit her.

"Are you fucking kidding me? Rapists don't have opportunities?"

13

"The Bookstore." Frankie says it conclusively. As I listen to her, I notice her shoulders. They're ever so slightly striated. Muscular but still feminine. I crave them lifting an arm toward me.

"Yeah. That could work. It never closes?"

"Nope."

"And we could always disperse to 2 Mile Surf Shop or the beach or, worst case, Smiley's."

"Yep."

"Good choice. It won't feel like some sort of organized revolt."

"Exactly. Plus, you think any of those fuckwads ever read a book?"

•

Heading downtown for a morning coffee, I take it all in. I wouldn't jaywalk in Brentwood. In Bolinas? I wouldn't hesitate to open a beer on the street and drink it in front of a cop. No one gives a fuck. About anything. And that heaviness adds to the gravity of this place. Does it feel freeing? Certainly. For a moment. But it's brief.

I skip the coffee and buy a six pack. Frankie's trick to pop the top off with the doorjamb works like a dream.

Liam.

He drives by, in his faded Ford Ranger. The truck bed is full of what appears to be a big shopping run in Marin. Bottles of booze. Chips. Sundries. Like he's throwing a party. Because he is.

He gives me a mad dog stare.

I return it.

He looks surprised. Surprised that I'd be so brazen after such an ass beating. But he's alone. And even if he might win, I'd welcome it.

My lack of fear breaks his stride. But then, he catches himself and motors off to the boat dock.

My own confidence takes me aback. For a moment. But it's not unlike hitting the guardrail on the freeway. Once you've hit it a few times, you no longer fear it. That's why the most confident drivers are the ones that have totaled a few cars. Importantly—they've totaled a few cars and walked away.

Dang it.

I spit out my second sip of KSA. I forgot that I've got kung fu in two hours.

•

Bruce Lee #5

A friend of mine joined CrossFit. He got stronger, more cut. But the most noticeable change? His confidence.

I asked him about it. "When I used to walk into a gym, I never knew what to do. Cardio? Some weights? Stretch? After three months at CrossFit, I didn't become the most ripped guy in the world, but I was trained. Now, I can walk into any gym, any hotel room or any prison cell and know what to do. I'm focused. I walk in, put my head down and go to work.

That same sensation is what martial arts does with fear. You still feel fear. You just know what to do with it. That training buys you time. Maybe it's only half a second. But it's enough. Enough time to react. To make a plan. To go to work.

●

"Really? You're laughing at me?" I set my phone and car keys into my cubby and enter the studio. Sifu Mark has already taken an inventory of my bruised face.

"You're gonna need a few more classes, George!"

"Maybe. But I didn't fight back. By choice."

"Outnumbered?!"

"Yep."

"Good job! Not fighting is the hardest!"

"Agreed."

"You OK? To work out?"

"Absofuckinglutely. Ooof. Sorry to swear, Sifu Mark."

"It's OK! Sometimes 'darnit' just doesn't cut it!"

I laugh.

"So what's on tap?"

"Today? Worst case scenario, kiddo!"

He kills the lights. Cranks awful music. It's pitch black.

He kicks me in the kidneys.

•

Disorientation. Mind numbing trance-techno sound. Random attacks. Chokes from behind. Kicks from the side. Leg sweeps directly in front of me—invisible, due to the blackness.

He spends three hours with me. Our longest session, by far. Repetition. Repetition. Repetition. Even if I don't become the oldest Navy Seal in US history, there's no attack he can approach that I don't have a response for. To protect myself. Or answer, with my own violence.

We finish.

I change back into jeans in the small, un-private studio. Grabbing my phone, on top of it sits half of an expired Bed Bath & Beyond coupon, with a short note written in the white space. In surprisingly precise penmanship, he's written an address and a four digit number: *7438.*

"Is this yours?"

"It's for you! A back up plan."

"For what?"

"George. You're a good kid. So honest! And most folks that come in here? They need something. More than just how to defend themselves. I think it's peace of mind? I dunno. You? One look at your face and anyone can tell you've got a lot on your plate!"

"It's that obvious, isn't it."

"Something's troubling you. I don't want to know! That's not my job! But you fight back way too hard. You need this too much, buddy."

It's painful how right he is.

"Sorry. I didn't mean to…"

"It's OK. You're in the right place. And that? That's as much as I can help. I'm sorry." He points to the paper. "It's in Monterey. My parents' old house. They passed a few years ago. We're remodeling it. But two of the bathrooms are done. No microwave, but the fridge works! Sometimes I drive down for a night just to drink beer by myself!"

"That sounds fantastic. Thank you for this."

"The key's in one of those real estate lockboxes. Pretty simple!"

"That's so kind. Thank you."

"Do me a favor, kiddo?"

"Anything."

"Commit that to memory? If anything happens, you didn't get that from me."

•

In the van, parked on yet another steep hill, I jot down notes in my iPhone. A super shorthand for the address. Basically a cryptogram, so that I don't betray him. Meet his request to not be an accomplice to my crime.

But the four digits. My thumb hits the phone icon.

7438.

7438.

I try to come up with a pneumonic device, using the letters assigned to each number on the keypad.

RID8?

PIEV?

SHET?

After eight tries, I realize that it's already there.

7438.

SIFU.

•

Turning onto the farm's long dirt driveway, Johnny blows by me. And guess who's in his passenger seat. Maya.

I'm tempted to stalk them, chase after them. But that's not an option in the big white puffy marshmallow this close to downtown. Instead, I'll just have to wait until Frankie gets back. Vent my fury on her.

Restless pacing won't help me; I may as well reconnect with TR.

From: Lewis, George

To: Rogers, Timothy

Subject: RE: Checking in on you

Tim—

Regarding your comment on not over-immersing myself—you've hit the nail on the head. As much as I love these escapades, I'm ready to settle down somewhere. Not sure exactly where, but certainly somewhere coastal and on this continent.

Let me know if you have any thoughts on the Bruce Lee #5 copy I sent this morning. For now, that should be a wrap with him. Very cool to learn kung fu and get paid for it. I do owe you one last surfing piece and will send that in the next few days.

Best,

George

"Hi!"

"Heeey."

"How was the city? You all arate'd out?" Frankie unpacks some groceries.

"It's kung fu. Jeet Kune Do, to be precise."

"Okaaay. Are you alright? You seem tense."

"I just saw Maya leave with Johnny. In his fucking truck."

"Yeah. They were going to Tomales Bay. To have oysters for lunch. I asked her to bring us back some."

"That doesn't bother you?"

"What?"

"The guy you hate. That we all hate. Being here. At your house. Taking Maya on a date?"

"I'm not. Are you jealous?"

"No! No. I don't know! Does it matter? We're attacking Johnny like it's the siege of Sarajevo. You're not worried at all that Maya is gonna tip him off?"

"Look. I hate that guy as much as you do. But you know how malleable Maya is. She broke it off with him. But he still keeps tabs on her. They have a relationship. I wish they didn't. But they do."

All I can do is shake my head.

"George. You don't understand Maya. She'd do anything to not be alone. Anything. In some ways, you've benefited from that."

"You're seriously comparing convenience canoodling to her shucking oysters with a felon?"

"Kinda? You're telling me you didn't knowingly make it convenient to make yourself available to Maya?"

"Ouch. That's brutal. I'm not saying it's false. But it's brutal."

"Do you ever try to get something you actually want, instead of accepting something that requires no effort?"

"I don't know, Frankie. Maybe? We all want to be desired. It doesn't always come with a lot of forethought."

"You didn't fore-think yourself into considering me first?"

"Is it a competition?"

"Fuck you, George."

I pause, trying to change the geo-location of our emotions. Of hers.

"Frankie, you're the most emotionally engaged person I've ever met. And incredibly thoughtful. And beautiful. And sometimes? Kind of a dick. But in a cool, stubborn, punch me and then give me a kiss kinda way." She softens. "The more I experience you, the more I am drawn to you. We can certainly talk about it more. But not today. Today, we have a higher purpose. We're trying to save some women that have no one fighting for them. I'm sure any of them would love to be in a nothing-fight with someone that cares about them right now, versus being sold off to a luxury boat full of techies."

"That's fair. We have a much bigger task than talking about us. But I reserve the right to bring it up again."

"Also fair."

She gives me a hard kiss and a bite. A peace offering that's meant to hurt a little. It does.

"Just chill on Maya and Johnny. There's nothing we can do about it. And there's some benefit to not alarming him the day before the deed. I don't think Maya will tell him a word. It threatens her self-preservation too much."

"I hope you're right. If not? We're fucked. Fuuucked."

"The house will be empty for two hours. Then I've gotta go to the bar. Do you wanna go surfing, or do you wanna take a nap?"

"I'm not sleepy."

"Stop being so literal, George." She nods toward the only room in the house I've not been invited into.

Hers.

•

Rude to check my emails while I'm on Frankie's bed and she's in the bathroom? Only if I get caught.

From: Rogers, Timothy
To: Lewis, George
Subject: Surf's up

George—

The last Bruce Lee piece was my favorite so far. A nice balance of intangible with practical. Try to do the same with your two remaining surfing pieces. That's right; you owe me two, not just one.

Nice to hear you want to settle down. No offense, but I'll believe it when I see it.

Best,

TR

"Which one of us is gonna tell Maya?"

"Um, neither of us?"

"Frankie. I don't want to do that."

"Trust me, she'll be relieved. We don't need to announce it. She's not stupid."

"I'm not saying she's stupid. Why would she be relieved?"

"I'm not sure why. Maybe her relationship with me? Maybe with everyone? She'd do anything to avoid a confrontation. So don't create one that doesn't need to happen, you sensitive little fucker."

"OK. OK. Geez."

"What would your game plan be? You want me to ask her? 'Hey Maya, how were the oysters? George just ate my clam! But you know his style, right? Does his dick always taste so salty?'"

"Jesus. Frankie…I just wanna…I just wanna be a decent guy. It's harder than you'd think."

"I don't doubt it. I really don't. But you need to see this for what it is. I'm not saying she's using you. But she's using you in the way girls use nice guys. She's lonely. You're lonely. You're a nice guy. Your dick gets hard. You like being doted on. You both get to skip a night alone."

"It's that transparent to you?"

"Yep."

"Yeeeah. You're right, I guess?"

"Go get us something to drink."

14

The back room at The Bookstore is unnervingly quiet, until Blake walks in with a cooler.

"Beer anyone? Seems illegal, but that's why we're here in the first place, right?"

"I'll take one."

"Me too."

"We'd better ice the rest. I didn't think they'd go so quick. Let me run and grab the other sixer in the truck."

Our small, anarchist group is assembling. The cold beers make it feel like a barbeque. Not a barbeque—a PTA meeting with a bar. But we have no PTA president. Time to prep my campaign speech.

Eminem uses the bathroom to prep for a battle. I use the Bolinas community urinal—aka anywhere outside. Especially the beach.

I walk back, kicking the sand off my feet and taking a look at

Blake's totems at 2 Mile Surf Shop. So cool. Maya pops up out of nowhere.

"Jesus!"

"Sorry."

"I wasn't expecting you."

"Beach bathroom?"

"Yeah, trashy?"

"Naw, you're a guy. Hey. Can I talk to you about something?"

"Johnny?"

"Yeeeah."

"How'd I guess? Because I saw you drive off with him."

She fidgets.

I stay silent.

"Sooo…" I nod, coaxing her to continue. "Johnny and I. We're still close. You know?"

"Yep." I nod. Grit my teeth. Just hearing her bring him up makes me furious, but I want to hear her out.

Her facial expressions tell me that she's still hooking up with him. Still intimate with him in some way. Who isn't in Bolinas?

I let her squirm.

"He's not irredeemable, you know?"

"Honestly, Maya. He is fucking irredeemable. That's why we're all here tonight. Did you forget that?"

"No! What they're doing is not OK! I'm fully supportive. Here."

She hands me a crumpled, hand-drawn map and timetable.

"Huh?"

"The boats. When they meet. Where they depart. And when."

"Holy shit. How do you have this? From today?"

"Yeah. I saw it in his truck. Copied it."

"And that was the only reason you went on a long lunch date with him? You knew you'd find something useful?"

"Does it matter?"

"Maya. Johnny cannot be your friend. Absolutely cannot. I love that you're giving me this. And it is immeasurably helpful. Huge. And I trust you." I lie. "But he is the worst type of felon. Type of human being. He preys on the weak. And everyone here tonight agrees. With the one, single exception of you."

She digests this. But it's clear she's too invested in him.

"You don't know him like I do. He's trying. So hard."

"Then why did you give me this?"

"I don't know! I don't know! It's not okay! OK? It's not. Those girls. Those women. No one should be treated like that. It's just. It's just Johnny. Johnny…he doesn't. He…he's just…he's better than that. I've been trying to show him…"

"Maya. Jesus fucking Christ."

"George. Just do what you've gotta do." She bats her fingers at her hand-drawn timeline and map. The fact that she drew it kills me. Such a personal betrayal by Johnny's biggest fan.

She turns and walks away.

●

Bolinas, CA—The Bookstore with no staff

Photo: Concerned citizens meet to discuss what? The first stoplight in Bolinas? Too

many stray cats? A fundraiser to build a new skate park?
@georgeous Pest control meeting. Beverages provided by @fortpointbeer

Maybe Maya's got a point. Do I think Johnny can reform? I dunno. Even if we are using the vagaries of maritime law to our advantage, and even if not a soul in town would miss whatever might happen to these idiots, we wouldn't be immune to any post-crime inquiries. I look over at Raj. He's tastefully dressed in a cardigan. He will break if questioned by police. I don't think he'd voluntarily give us up. But the intensity would crush him. Break his spirit. Do I want to stick a big fat speedbump in front of this trafficking ring? Absolutely. Does risking traumatizing Raj make me rethink if it's worth it? It does. But only for a second. I still land on the same spot. Fuck those clowns.

I walk back into The Bookstore. Blake hands me a fresh beer, as if it's the microphone.

"Everyone cool with the plan?"

"Yep." Blake adds an affirmative nod. It's his boat. He has the greatest risk, besides me.

"Let's recap, while we're all together. Blake you drop me off. I swim under the boat. Snip snip, disable boat. I swim toward shore. You swing back and pick me up. The shore team radios it in, as soon as we confirm and they have a visual on the second boat."

"I'm sure Raj knows to wait, until he has 'a visual'." Frankie retreads my word choice. Not malicious. A tease. The kind you start giving your new boyfr…never mind.

We pause. Blake nods again.

"It's good. Simple. And probably the best call. Worst case? We get a misdemeanor for destruction of property, trespassing." He looks to the crew for confirmation, and he gets it. "You're gonna need a surfboard. A longboard. You can paddle twice as fast as you can swim. It's less thrashy, both for sharks and anyone with their eyes on the water, as you approach and exit."

"A nine-foot, bright white surfboard?"

"I have a black one."

"Hmmm. I feel way stronger as a swimmer, than paddling a board."

"Get over it. Plus, you're gonna need some tools. Wire cutters. Maybe a saw. Some back up stuff. Just in case."

"Like what?"

"Chemlights. So I can find you. Flares wouldn't be a bad idea. You'll need a backpack. A small one. But swimming with a backpack is cumbersome." He takes a swig. "The longboard? That's why."

Blake has a natural swagger. It makes me wonder how to acquire my own.

"Frankie? You cool?" I'm tempted to interrupt and ask if she's disappointed that we're not using her totally infeasible homemade fertilizer bomb brainchild. But it's not a good time.

"Indeed. The boat with the techie guys will leave from Bolinas Lagoon. The girls will come in another boat. Johnny and crew do this to hedge their bets. Minimize the exposure. So that both boats are only together for the sex fest. But it's to our advantage. The girls coming on a small boat means they're probably only guarded by one or two guys.

We call in the boat distress. Customs. Homeland Security. Every single agency we can think of. Including the Marin Sherriff's Department. A little overkill, but so many agencies will have the same info, no one will be able to ignore it. There won't be much resistance, if any, to scoop the girls. The guys will probably drop them like a bad habit."

"That is solid." Blake turns to Raj. "Beer?"

"Oh, no thank you. I'm drinking Prosecco." He is. From a stemless plastic wine glass he apparently keeps on his person.

•

"Will your cell phones work, reliably? While you're at sea?" Raj asks the question that I should have thought to ask.

"Probably, but we shouldn't use them." Blake is right. Has he committed high seas crimes before?

"Yeah, we don't want our calls documented with time stamps and GPS. It'd be evidence, if anyone gets arrested. And the first thing they subpoena nowadays? Cellphone data."

"We'll just use the boat's VHF radio."

"VHS?"

"VHF. Stands for Very High Frequency. Raj, use channel 19. And speak very, very little. When you see the girls arrive at the dock, just mention whether the sails are up or down. Up for go. Down for no go. I'll confirm, and we'll leave it at that. Frankie, keep this one with you." He hands her an oversized walkie-talkie.

"Just use it to listen. Channel 16 is the distress channel." Frankie nods. But he's not saying it to her. He's saying it for the benefit of the rest of us. "It's monitored twenty-four hours a day by the Coast Guard and all commercial vessels. If something is up, you'll hear about it. If not, you'll hear Raj radio the Coast Guard on the same channel. In either scenario, head over to meet Raj at the dock. The girls will be a lot calmer, with another female there. He'll be on my buddy's boat, The Anaconda."

Frankie is standing next to me. She mumbles, just so I can hear.

"My anaconda don't want none..."

I shake my head in fake disappointment. A quick, subtle comedic break shared between two...lovers? I'm not sure what to call us. But it doesn't matter. Frankie knows her audience.

Blake continues, all business.

"Frankie, keep in mind, you're just the lookout. Keep your eyes open around town, too." Can I have her job?

Raj handles the walkie talkie.

"Blake, if the sails tell you the position of the girls, what about if we need you to abort. Get you and George back. Or if there's danger?"

"Yeah. Good point. Just mention the ballast. The ballast is cracked. The ballast is broken. If you say anything negative about the ballast, we'll pull out."

•

In the living room of the van, I'm wracking my brain, trying to come up with one of the last surfing pieces. But I'm too distracted. The plan. The timing. All of it. It's complex. And it's simple. It's too small of a gesture, and it's just right. And all of us doing it, something about that is so heartwarming, it helps me let a lot of the other stuff go.

"Aaah!"

"Sorry!"

"You scared the fuck out of me."

"You're the one that made me come out to you. Why aren't you in the house?"

"Maya is pissed at me."

"Don't be so self-absorbed. She's at work."

"I know. But…I dunno. It's time for me to go, you know?"

"And I'm guessing you're leaving tomorrow?"

"Yeah. Tomorrow seems smartest, right?"

"I figured. I don't want that. But I figured that's what your plan was."

We pause for a sec. I consider grabbing two beers from my cooler. But I don't want to challenge her seriousness. I close my computer screen and set it on the cooler.

"Can we talk?" She locks eyes with me.

"We are talking."

"I want to change the plan."

"Why?"

"Not the logistics. Well, some."

"Oh god. What?"

"Number one? Blake is out."

"No!"

"Yep. I already told him."

"Why?"

"He's getting married in a month. He is fully entrenched here. A Bolinas lifer. We'll still use his boat, but he'll be safely home with his lady. Full alibi and arm's length from me."

"Ugh."

"I just texted him about taking his lady to Smiley's. Keep an eye out. Backup to the backup plan."

I am not pleased. Although, eyes on Smiley's isn't the worst idea.

"Why are you tinkering with this at the eleventh hour?"

"Because I want to do it. I don't want to be a bystander."

"You're not a bystander. Your role is crucial."

"It's done, George."

"Ugh." I stew for a moment. "I'm annoyed. But also relieved. We'll lose a lot in Blake's competence. You sure you feel comfortable captaining…"

"Are you fuckin serious? I can drive a boat, George. I can handle it. Trust me."

"I do. And knowing you'll be my side comforts me. I mean it."

"Me too." She leans over and kisses my forehead. "And one more thing."

"What."

"I don't know how we'd do it, exactly, but I want to kill those cocksuckers."

•

"Frankie, let it go."

"No way."

"Are you seriously asking why aren't we killing them?"

"Yeah! That's the whole point! They aren't just criminals, they are fucking destroying lives! They don't deserve to live."

"I know. I know. And I agree. But, Frankie, incapacitating a boat is one thing. Blowing it up and killing a few dudes? I'm not qualified. And who am I to judge? Johnny? For sure. Liam? I'd like to execute him with my own bare hands. But the techie guys? What if that was their first mistake? It's for me to decide that they should die? Because someone coaxed them into a sex cruise? It's too extreme."

"Are you backing off because of Maya?"

"I'm not. I think she may be under Johnny's thumb, but she's right. I am not a professional mercenary. All of you guys still need to live in Bolinas. We can't create some sort of irrecoverable catastrophe. It's too much."

"Uuugh."

"Frankie. Disabling their boat and stealing their girls is enough! It is a step! It says, 'Fuck off guys. This aggression will not stand!'"

"Will not stand, man." She laughs. Then looks at her feet. "It's just…I fucking hate that these guys will get away without any consequences. Maybe we'll stop them. For now. But they'll never be punished for what they've done. It's wrong."

"And we're doing something about it. It's not going to solve everything. But it's something. We've got to be satisfied."

"Yeah. I guess. I'm still pissed. But you're the only person that's actually doing something. So I can't be pissed at you."

"Even though you are."

"I so am!"

She punches me. Hard. I respond with a long drawn-out hug. I want to kiss her, but I don't want to undermine her sincerity.

"You're never gonna be able to sleep. Come, come watch a movie with me in bed."

"But when Maya gets home…" I really want her to answer this for me.

"Fuck Maya. She bailed. She treats you like shit, anyway."

•

Why didn't I tell Frankie that I'm not completely opposed to killing them, too? Or that I probably wouldn't stand in the way of a very convenient and possibly lethal accident? If the opportunity presents itself, I'm not sure what I will do, but I'm certainly open to both of those fuckers disappearing.

It's a pretty significant omission. But I didn't tell Frankie for two reasons: 1) I'm still not sure where I stand on such an extreme measure and 2) plausible deniability. She won't need to lie about something she never knew about.

Regardless, their boat? I will be blowing it up. But not with some homemade gadget. Every vehicle with fuel and/or a kitchen is its own stick of dynamite.

15

Bolinas has the best spooning weather on earth. It's always cool, the air perpetually moist. It's cold enough that a warm body always feels perfect. But it's not so cold that it's unbearable. Year-round fall weather makes you want to live in bed.

Frankie is watching *The Walking Dead*. I'm not a zombie guy, so it could be season two or season nine. She pauses it. Yes, an actual hold-in-your-hand DVD.

"George. Come lay on me."

"OK?"

"I just wanna feel your weight."

"No need to sell it."

•

5am.

We fell asleep. And then woke. And then had hazy, sexy-time. The perfect combination of twilight, dozing and feeling warm and connected.

But it fully wakes me up.

"Are you awake, awake?"

"Ummph." Frankie's sleepy sigh is more of a growl.

"Can't sleep."

"Go surfing." It's good advice. And she gives it without lifting her head from the pillow.

"OK." I kiss her shoulder.

"First, go make coffee. Gimme a sec to wake up, and I'll go with you." She rolls over to put an extra period on this sentence.

"Done."

There's nothing like having sex and then immediately transitioning into something else. Spooning and cuddling are great. But sometimes you just want to knock one out and then crush some errands. Or go surfing. Or fight crime. I find this all-business vibe about Frankie very sexy.

I set water on the stove and head to the van for fresh grounds.

Passing Maya's room, the door's wide open. A lonely cat lies across her bed and stares at me, wishing I was someone else. She didn't come home last night. I'm both relieved and alarmed.

•

I finish making coffee and deliver a light sugar, light cream batch to Frankie. Her body doesn't stir. Not immediately. But she can smell it. She rolls over. Slowly.

"Mmm." She takes a cautious sip.

"No Maya. She didn't come home."

"Yeah. She would have at least said hello. But probably no threesome, again. Given that you're looking to ice her ex-boyfriend."

"We. We are looking to ice. And it's more like thwart. You with the killing! Let it go."

"We." Another coffee sip. "Do you think, if given another week, you might fuck the cats, too? Sorry we don't have a third roommate for you to bed."

"Jesus."

"Truth hurt?"

"Always. Why are the fangs out?"

She pauses. Blows on her coffee. Which doesn't need it. Because I made it the perfect temperature.

She pulls the covers around her.

"Our coffee boy is gonna be gone tomorrow, and I'm pretty bummed about it. Even if he only gives me coffees meant for Maya."

"Frankie. I know that this has all been a bit weird, but I'm super into you."

"And you're leaving tonight."

"This situation? Yes. This location? Yes. For a bit. You? I hope not. Plus, aren't you going to be right behind me, heading to your dad's in Buellton?"

"Yeah. But only for a week or two. Not forever. I need to come back. And Bolinas to LA is a seven hour drive."

"About three and change, if we split it. San Luis Obispo?"

"Don't tease."

"Two weeks. San Luis Obispo. Meet me there. There's a mustard yellow motel off the Marsh Street exit. Across from the Chevron. Can't remember the name, but it's the only one. I saw it when I got gas. Only one story. Vending machines. Basic."

"Are you serious? Really? I love SLO."

"Dead serious."

We kiss. Start to fondle. But I don't want to get lost in our bodies. I do really dig her.

"It'll be easy. You're only off weekdays, right?"

"I could schedule myself off two days back to back. But they'd have to be a Monday and a Tuesday. Sorry—a weekend is not an option."

"It's better. I work almost 100% remote. No traffic. No tourists. More time to…"

"Scout another chick we can have a threesome with?"

"That's the best thing about threesomes. They always come with no strings."

•

Frankie paddles toward me. Back from a wave I couldn't have ridden. At least not yet.

"Incredible wave. And you dominated it. Do you ever approach anything without intensity?"

"Do you ever not analyze every single moment?"

"Fair point."

"I hate it when you do that."

"What?"

"Respond to me being mean with something honest. It's off-putting. Be an asshole. At least more consistently?"

"I am."

"I know. Hee hee hee." She looks over my shoulder. "Go go go!"

Roommate. Surf coach. Possible girlfriend. I do what I'm told.

The waves are good. Really good. Of course they are. Because we have no time.

A near perfect right. Not that big but super clean. I paddle back to her, all smiles.

"You're getting better!"

"Thank you. I'm seriously falling in love with this sport."

She grins, turns and takes off on a bomb. My next surfing vignette comes to me.

Surfing #4

If writing is like painting with words, then reading is like painting with a friend.
--Anonymous

Surfing with friends? It's like going to your favorite movie. Except you get to star in it.

Chatting. Keeping your eyes on the horizon. Something we rarely do, but surfing reminds us how important it is to see what is coming our way. And surfing purifies it, because it adds hope. Hope that a wave will come that the two of us can share. A perfect A-frame, "You go right! I'll go left!"

Growing up in Southern California, we always lived inland. In Pasadena. But surf culture was everywhere. I knew, someday, that I'd try it. Scratch that. I knew I'd become obsessed. Maybe that's why I held out so long.

Of the thousands of bumper stickers I saw, on pickup trucks and Hondas with roof racks heading west on the 10, one stands out as my favorite. It's from a defunct surf apparel brand called Instinct: Waiting for Waves is OK. Most People Spend their Lives Waiting for Nothing.

•

We walk back in a brief moment of bliss. Before our huge day. Before we sever our burst of close proximity love and try to keep it tethered from hundreds of miles away. I'd be happy to let it lie, but Frankie is not.

"George. You're such an enigma."

"International man of mystery?"

"Nah, I just kind of wonder why you came here?"

"To Bolinas?"

"To anywhere. You're always on these big sojourns. Seeking or running. I dunno. Looking for something. And you do them alone. But you are so lonely."

"Uhhh."

"I mean, you're fine. You're independent. Self-sufficient. Don't get me wrong, it's super cool. Sexy even. But it seems so opposite of what you're all about. You know?"

"I think?" I can tell she's more curious than combative. I try to keep from getting defensive. It's hard. "I think loneliness is the human condition. It's always seeping into the cracks. Even when we're surrounded by other people. I try to keep doing what I'm doing and not get crushed by it."

She thinks about it.

"That makes sense. It does. But do you listen when you talk?"

"That's really the only time I listen. Maybe with the one exception of my mother. If being constantly distracted while trying to listen counts."

"I'm serious, you fucker."

"OK. OK."

"Panama, Australia, here. Everything you talk about is other people. Your friend PJ. That bitch Shawna you used to date. P.S. Even if we don't work out, if you go back to her, I'll fucking kill you."

"Yeah. Apparently no one is a fan of Shawna."

"But to listen to you talk about her? Craig-oh? Everyone. Your whole mind-space revolves around people. You entrench. Then you bail. Or run. Or go adventuring. Why do you do that?"

•

We shower together. But it's too soon. It's too intimate. It's something you do after dating for a month. Not a day and a half.

After some kissing, we wash each other in a loving but efficient way. Almost platonically. Almost.

"Why do you scrub my entire body like a truck, then treat my dick like a broken piece of China? The caution is appreciated, but the difference is stark."

"How is one supposed to wash balls? It's like trying to write your name on a water balloon!"

"Wow. That's good. Can I use that?"

"In an article? Yes!"

She knocks out her lady parts and backdoor in a smooth, subtle way that tempts me to ask her for a repeat.

"Again? Seriously?"

"What?"

"My tits!"

"I was washing them?"

"They're clean. Right now, they're the cleanest part of my body."

•

"What's up, Raj?"

"Monsieur Georges. Comment allez-vous?"

"Je vais bien. Are you wearing a cravat?"

"Oui."

"I don't even know how to spell that word."

"Me neither!" He guffaws. Another difficult word to spell.

"I love how fancy you are. Especially in Bolinas. It's bold. Brave."

"Monsieur Georges, if you don't put the collar on the dog, it doesn't know it's going for a walk."

•

Raj has the phone number for every law enforcement agency in North America, pinned to a corkboard in the back of The Bookstore. Our black ops war room.

Before gracefully exiting our mission, Blake posted our departure, reconnoiter and exit routes—drawn with artistic precision—on a massive piece of pegboard. Oh, and the keys to his boat. And his black longboard. Such a solid guy. Frankie's boat diagram is taped up next to Blake's map, with the fuel lines I'm supposed to cut, circled with a blue highlighter bought from Staples. It's oddly beautiful. I'd love to have the whole thing in my future apartment as art, if it wasn't evidence.

Frankie's in the zone. She hands me a backpack.

"Here. Try this on." Frankie hands it to me, dangling from a carabiner.

"Every backpack needs at least one carabiner."

"Yep. And surely you have ten more stashed in that van of yours, if one is not enough." She's not wrong.

"It's heavy."

"Tools and fins."

"Fins? And a surfboard?"

"They're Da Fins. They float. They'll help float the backpack. Just in case you lose the board. Plus the tools are heavy. Dikes and a saw. It's overkill, but we only have one shot."

"Smart. But still, the fins? They're so bulky."

"Just in case."

"In case what?"

Raj pipes up.

"She means in case she gets caught. Or you get caught. Or something happens to the board. Just in case. Oui, chef?"

"OK. OK. Oui."

"Monsieur Georges, be very, very careful. The commotion of whatever you do on the water. Cutting the lines. The electrical. Whatever. I'm not sure if it will deter or draw predatory fish. But you do not want to be in the water for long after. Not on a board. Not with fins. Just get to the boat, do your thing and get out of there."

"Did you just watch *Sharknado* or something?"

Frankie smiles and adds a little levity.

"I know you're a SoCal boy. You may not be aware of our proximity to the Farallon Islands. There are more great whites here right now than anywhere else on earth. The landlord is always stopping by, unannounced."

•

Plan. Plan. Plan.

Frankie does this. Raj does that.

But most of it? In the end? I have to do it.

And that's fine by me.

•

Frankie is at work. She's gonna close early. Knowing it will be quiet. Knowing the boys chose a weekday to host their sex cruise, because it's less suspicious. No delayed weekend warrior fishing charters passing by. And none of them will be at Smiley's. Otherwise, there'd be a high likelihood that Johnny and Liam might have bent elbows until last call. Spending their hard earned cash.

The kickoff doesn't start until after sunset anyway. The Silicon Valley guys have to finish writing code. Finish finance spreadsheets. Finish commuting via WiFi enabled glamour buses. Finish being the kind of guys who don't support sex trafficking.

•

Unable to concentrate, I further diminish my attention span by checking Instagram. A quick scroll tells me that technology has given us the one true narcissistic analytic: the selfie-ratio. I'm too proud to make the same comment about the inspirational quote ratio, because...

San Francisco, CA— Chinatown, the birthplace of Bruce Lee
Photo: Bruce Lee kicking an invisible adversary, watermarked behind his foot: If you spend too much time thinking about a thing, you'll never get it done.
@georgeous Giddy up. @frankiethetankie @iminlouvre @totemsandfloatems

Ring, ring.
"George?"
"Hey mom."
"Are you OK?"
"Yeah. Why?"
"We haven't spoken twice in twenty days, since you were in high school."
"I know. That's kinda terrible. I'm gonna try to fix that. I'll be back home in a couple days."
"You always go on a self-improvement kick, whenever you break up with Shawna."
"Mom!"
"It's true."
"We weren't even back together, so…"
"You saw her on Christmas. And I'm guessing you've not talked to her since?"
"You are ruthless."

"And correct?"

"Ugh. Yes."

"I'm sorry sweetie. I know how much you love her. I really, really like her, too. You two were just so...intense all the time. Plus, she...well...how many advisors did she end up going through? During her PhD?"

"Four."

"Exactly. She's a lovely girl. An absolute heart of gold. Just seems a bit enchanted with chaos. Hopefully she'll grow out of it."

"Totally. I used to think that a tornado a thousand miles away could find her. But after the fifteenth one hit, I had to at least consider..."

"That you were dating the eye of the tornado."

"Yep."

"Oh, sweetie. I'm sorry. That must be hard. But you need to keep in mind, you're no summer breeze yourself."

From: Lewis, George

To: Rogers, Timothy

Subject: Surfing #4

Tim—

You are right.

I owe you two more surfing vignettes. I have one written, and I'll send it right after a quick proofread.

The last one may have a slight delay. I'm heading back to LA in the next few days. I'd like to do the last one a little closer to home.

I hope that works.

Warmly,

George

16

The Bolinas People's Store simultaneously has nothing and everything. I'm elated to find a single carabiner with a 200lb test weight. I was restless and decided to replace Blake's well-worn one. Neurotic? Indeed. Pointless? Not necessarily. Just doing this errand is keeping my mind occupied. And I take solace in knowing that all of his gear isn't going to fall off the boat and sink to the bottom of the ocean, before I get a chance to use it.

"Just this, sweetheart? No fun-juice?" I smile at her attempt at an upsell. The embroidered pot leaf on her cardigan tells me that she won't need to push $30 bottles of mediocre chardonnay, as soon as they get their recreational cannabis sales license.

"No, thank you."

•

Jumping into the van, I head home, to see if I can sneak in a nap.

At the crossroads, I look to my right to check for oncoming traffic. But I see the trunk of Maya's hand-me-down Mercedes. Hardly a Bolinas surf-mobile.

Without thinking, I follow. She's driving much faster than expected. Twice as fast as her normal tempo on foot. I keep my distance, as I have a pretty good guess where she's headed.

Team Brolinas shacks up at a decrepit compound outside of town. I've heard the echoing sound of them partying a few nights, on my way back from San Francisco.

She bangs a hard right onto a dirt road. It's next to a seasonal fruit stand that surely doubles as a drug sale meet up spot in the winter. We're at the foothills, so it can't be far inland.

I park behind the stand.

Red lights.

She's stopped.

Close. Maybe 200 feet down the road.

I head toward her, keeping out of sight in the trees and brush that line the unpaved driveway.

"This is fucking ridiculous." I whisper a self-critique of this recon mission, as it is fucking ridiculous.

Maya exits her car, pulling a big overnight bag out. She's in sweats, but her hair is up, and she has makeup on. A lot of makeup. She looks like Cleopatra on the way to Pilates.

Out come the girls. And Johnny. Johnny stays on the porch.

"Dude, you're not even gonna grab her bag?" Another whisper to myself stating the obvious.

The three girls almost run to her.

Hugs.

Some fawning over her hair.

As if they're welcoming their cool young aunt that they admire.

Welcoming their…friend.

•

Most nights I sleep but do not rejuvenate. Because even if I don't have an actual nightmare, my dreams are filled with turmoil. They were always intense, but my recent life experiences have ratcheted this up. A lot. I would not have chosen this—to never really sleep. But it has its benefits. Nightmares remind us that waking up is a gift. And to not take ourselves too seriously. Much bigger problems are out in the world, as well as hiding in our subconscious.

The other reminder is to nap. Especially when everything in the outside world feels inconceivable. Take a nap and start over. As often as possible. Naps are where the real rest comes from.

"GEORGE!"

"Uh, wha?"

"Are you fucking sleeping?"

"No, I…working. Was…what time is it?"

"George! Fuck!"

"What? I? I'm just…"

"Is your wetsuit dry?"

"Oh, yeah."

"Go get it. We need to leave in twenty minutes."

"We?"

"I'm gonna drive us, jacktard. You want to leave your van at the docks? Duh?"

"Oh, right. Good call. Thanks."

She shakes her head.

"I can't believe you were sleeping. It's absurd."

"I haven't slept normal in days. I nap when I'm stressed. Maybe I'm a highly functioning narcoleptic? Sorry. Are you legit mad at me?"

She sighs. Looks down.

"George. I'm scared."

"So am I. More than you'd think."

"Really?"

"I saw Maya."

"OK."

"I followed her. I don't know why. I just did it. She went out to Johnny's."

"So?"

"No, check it out. All of the girls are there. That's where they live, apparently."

"Oh, god."

"It gets worse. Maya was all dolled up. Like full-blown hairdo. Caked with makeup."

"Ew."

"And she KNOWS them. The girls! Like she's their friend or madame or something."

"Or another captive. But she's just got a leash that extends to this farm."

"Yep. How fucked up is that?"

"It's super fucked up. But it's also not surprising. She's clearly got Stockholm Syndrome. We need to save her, too."

"Could not agree more. Ugh."

"Are you sure you still wanna do this?"

"Frankie, we've talked about it a million times."

"You're creating two new enemies that value life at zero. You're doing a pretty dangerous task. FYI—it's illegal. It's all coming to a head, and part of me is finally realizing that it's absolutely insane. Is it really worth it?"

"Yep. But are you sure you know how to drive a boat? Super-duper sure?"

"I can drive a boat, dick."

"OK. Sorry."

"Who do you think got it all gassed up and ready?"

I smile and pull her in for a hug. She relents. Softens. Whispers in my ear.

"The Avenue Inn."

"Huh?"

"The place. In SLO. The motel."

"Oh, right! That's it!"

"I found it. Right across from Chevron, like you said. I'll text it to you. Monday and Tuesday. Two weeks. I made a reservation." She looks up at me, tentative. Like she went too far. Wondering how I'll react.

"Perfect. Do you know the surf spots around there?"

"I'm trying to see if you want to be with me, and you wanna know what the waves are like. Awesome."

"I owe my boss one more surfing vignette. I was hoping to do a little combo."

"Ugh. OK. There's Montana de Oro. But if you want a good story, the guys in Morro Bay paddle across the harbor, walk a mile and surf the south Jetty. They call it The Triathlon."

"Done. Then let's go to Sycamore Hot Springs. Maybe Esquire will pay for us to get massages, for research."

"That's a pretty good save, fucker."

•

"Your truck is filthy."

"Fuck you. You've lived with us for free for three weeks. You could've washed it anytime you wanted."

"Where? At the Bolinas Super Car Wash? Or just on your dirt driveway, by hand with a toothbrush from the grocery store that sells only one type of toothbrush." She smiles. I kiss her neck. "Don't get all cranky at me, because you're getting separation anxiety."

She grabs my hand and squeezes it. She's not one for holding hands. I'm glad. Because mine are softer than hers.

We share a perfect moment. Passing through downtown, I stroke her forearm. I'm glad we have a plan. Not the crime. The motel. Knowing I'll get to see Frankie again makes me sweet on this place. Makes me thankful for Bolinas.

But it's brief.

Because it gets interrupted.

"Oh, man."

It's Johnny and Liam and Pretty Boy. Plus all the girls.

It's confounding whether or not to call them women. They're so young. But based on life experience, they're definitely adults. Yet, it feels insensitive to prematurely age them—based on life choices made for them. For the moment, I'll stick with girls. Until I'm inevitably corrected.

"Holy fuck."

We watch Liam double tap Johnny's hood and then hop in his own truck, with Pretty Boy riding shotgun. All of the broey stickers on the back glass don't hide the girls sitting in the back jump seats of each truck.

Johnny blows by us. Nods. Meanly. With a half-smile but gritting his teeth. His front seat passenger looks straight ahead. Not returning our stares but feeling them.

Maya.

Now, fully dressed like a Barbie doll.

•

"Maya was with them?" Raj's big eyes pop behind fashion reading glasses that do not appear to have a prescription.

"Yep. Looking like she'll be another entertainer." I say this as a matter of fact, but to call it a mindfuck would be an understatement.

"Merde. Quite unexpected. Should we back off?"

I think about it. Look at Frankie. She locks eyes with me.

"That little fucker. She's fucking us. George, we can't…"

"No, no, I know. There's no way we can put Maya in any jeopardy.

Zero. I say we move forward with the plan. If she's there, we bail. Live to fight another day."

•

Out on the boat, it's beautiful.

"Dude! You're taking photos?!" Frankie barks.

"It's so pretty, I…"

"Turn your phone OFF. Stick it in MY bag. You can have it in a few hours. Come on, George. Stay focused."

"Sorry. I don't know why I'm so spacey. Let me put my wetsuit on."

"Good idea." She says it with the frustration of a mom that finally gets her way but can't enjoy it.

Frankie's a natural boat captain. All that's missing is the hat.

I turn my phone on Airplane Mode and quickly jot down a few notes for a potential Instagram, before turning it off.

Pacific Ocean, CA
Photo: The sun setting into a field of clouds over the ocean.
@georgeous Sunset is the best time to remember that you should be planning your ride home before it gets dark. @uber

"Let's check in on these kiddies."

"Anaconda, come in."

A pause on the line. I swear I hear Raj fumble it. His hands are probably slippery from snacking on a buttered baguette.

"Yes? Uh, yes. Copy!"

He's so excited; it's a little charming.

"Checking in on the sails. Over."

"The sails are up! All good!" He takes a breath, about to say something, but exhales and gives a nervous, "Over!"

"The ballast?"

"Copy!" Apparently, Raj did not have a lot of toys as a child. Frankie shrugs, but she is, at her core, a professional.

"Anaconda. Please provide the status of the ballast. Over."

"Oh! Copy! Wait. I mean not copy?"

"Anaconda. Is the ballast cracked, or does it look OK?"

"Oh, no! The ballast is great!"

Jesus Raj.

"Copy. Hail me a Crab, over and out."

That's right. Blake's boat is named *Hail me a Crab*.

•

I put on the wetsuit. It feels nice; the air off the water is chilly. Frankie pulls out two beers and a tackle box.

"That's what I'm talkin' about."

"Huh?"

"A beer. To take the edge off. You know. Before I go destroy a perfectly good boat?"

"No dummy. They're props. If the Coasties come, we're just a normal couple sipping beers, hoping a tuna bites."

"Or a salmon. I love salmon."

"NOT a salmon. And don't say that. Salmon's not in season."

"Oh. Sorry."

"Jesus, George. A seaman, you're not. Thank god you're a swimmer."

"I'll be fine. And I don't know what to call it, but I am so used to being in charge, whenever I get around someone that knows what they're doing, I tend to check out. Apologies. It's annoying."

"Competency Proximity Disorder."

"Is that what it's called?"

"No, dude. I just made that up. Hand me that monocular."

I look around. Whatever she's looking for is invisible.

"The thing that looks like half a set of binoculars."

"Why didn't you just say that?"

"Because that's not what it's called."

"Here you go, Super Literal Woman." I hand it over.

"I see boat number one. Fuck. Fuck."

"What?"

"It's got two outboard motors."

"Oh no. Fuuuck." The last word I whisper, and it lingers.

"It's not the same boat."

"Are you sure it's them?"

"They're literally sitting on the X on Maya's map."

"Maybe they replaced the inboard with two outboards?" I'm grasping at straws.

"Nope. That boat is brand spanking new. Practically still has the price tag on it. Business can't be that good. Johnny must have every penny to his name in that thing. Those motherfucking assholes."

"Oh man. I guess it doesn't really matter? I'll have to figure something out, no matter what. Stick with the plan, right?" I say this with a little less confidence than I'd hoped.

"Yep. You're just gonna have to be more creative."

"OK. We can always abort. How far away is it?"

"It's gotta be…in nautical miles…eh, never mind. Say it's a mile from us, then another 2 miles from shore. Roughly. Here, look at the rock formation on the shore that looks like a fist, just to the right of that, about halfway between us and the shore."

She hands me the thing I want to call a periscope.

"See them?"

"No…wait…" I pop my eyes up and reorient myself. "OK. Yeah. I see them. Man, this thing would be awesome for checking the surf."

"I know, right?" Her eyes light up. "Especially at Pt. Reyes or down at Killers north of Cayucos, where the break is a ¼ mile out. That's just outside of SLO."

"We're on an undercover mission and you're planning our long weekend? I love it."

"Fuck you! You wanna drive this boat?"

"Hey! I was being serious. Plus, I didn't even blink when you said, 'couple'. Chill."

"No, you didn't. OK." She goes back into boat captain mode. "The boat. It's staying in the same spot?"

"Yep. Where did they get that thing? It's a monster."

"I'm not sure if they dropped it into the water from a boat launch or what. But where you want to keep your eyes is on the lagoon, where the girls are coming from. Look. If we're headed toward twelve o'clock,

the lagoon is about two thirty. If you see the girls, don't do anything
dramatic."

"Like blow up the boat?"

"Like blow up the fucking boat."

"Why do we keep talking about this?"

"Why do you pretend that zero percent of you, ZERO percent,
isn't considering something more drastic?"

"Frankie..."

"Don't fucking lie to me! You haven't even joked once about
killing these guys. Not once. That's how I know you're hiding
something. It better be to protect me, because I'm gonna be
FUCKING PISSED if you're keeping a secret this big from me."

"You're already pissed."

"George. Own it."

"OK. Jesus. I've been considering it. But only if the opportunity is
perfect. OK?"

"Agreed. Of course. But if it is, take it. OK? If we have to flee to
Mexico, I'm in."

"So you're committed?" I jab. I can't help it. I'm nervous.

"I put flares in your backpack. I'm committed."

"Wow. Thank you?"

"You're welcome."

•

"Ready?"

"Yep."

We've waited about an hour. Thank god I have the wetsuit on, because I really didn't pack warm enough. It's cold. But the sky is clear. And Johnny's boat is unmistakable in the distance. With all the light they're giving off, it'll make it nearly impossible for anyone inside the boat to see us. More importantly, to see me.

We're at a spot that's roughly half a mile from Johnny's boat. The paddle looks far. Frankie cut the lights ages ago, and the sun has long set. She's got the throttle low; it's almost inaudible.

From here, Johnny's boat looks like a floating casino. A beacon for the girls. I grab the monocular and can detect one person moving inside. Just one.

Frankie kills the motor.

Silence.

"Water is calm. Not a cloud in the sky. Now it's up to us. Or actually, you George. Most of my work is done."

"I know. I'm good."

"Look at the moon."

"OK?"

"Just listen. The moon. It'll travel that direction." Her finger traces a medium-low arc in the sky. "I'm going to head further out to sea. Keeping myself between the moon and you. The moon will move a little but not that much."

"Cool. Got it."

"It'll be really hard to see you. So be careful. Don't let me hit you. If you can wave something that would be ideal. But I won't count on it."

"What if all I have are the fins?"

"Waving a fin is better than nothing. But Blake also gave us ChemLights." She hands them over. "Slide these next to your forearms inside your wetsuit. Break one and wave it at me. Maybe keep one as a spare."

"Glow sticks? Kinda brilliant. Kinda EDM concert."

"They work. And they're waterproof."

"You are amazing. I'm so glad you're here."

She smiles. But we don't have time for a kiss.

"George, be really careful, OK? I know you're a great swimmer, but we're in the open ocean. Every backup plan involves you paddling, kicking with fins or straight up swimming back to Bolinas. You totally understand that, right?"

"I do. But you said it's less than two miles to Bolinas. To the north side. That looks about right."

"Under two nautical miles. But two standard miles is close enough. Add currents, creatures. It's a long swim."

"I know."

"Are you sure?"

"I'm sure. I appreciate your meticulousness. I'm good."

"If you need to, light a flare from the boat. I will come immediately. I won't take my eyes off you. I promise." Most humans would cry right now. Not Frankie. She's got ovaries of steel. "Even if I can't see you, I will not stop looking. OK?"

"I'm good. I swear. OK?"

"OK." She examines my gear. In the interim, I've put on the backpack, tucked the glow sticks and set the pitch-black surfboard in the corner of the boat—ready to go.

"Look at those guys. Totally oblivious." She stares at Johnny's boat. "What are they playing? The Frat Rock soundtrack?"

"Whatever it is, it sounds awful."

"Idiots. Not paying attention." I grab the board and lift my leg over the back of the boat. She pauses me, with a hand on my chest. "One sec, lemme get you closer. With that set up, they won't notice a goddamn thing."

•

"Why does it look like Liam's alone? I know the girls are coming in the other boat. But he's totally alone? No Johnny? No Maya? No techies?"

Frankie cuts me off.

"Dunno. Doesn't matter. You need to jump in. And I need to get out of here."

I put the leash on, check my glow sticks, pull the backpack taut and clip the chest strap. The chest strap is the stupidest thing on a backpack—directly compressing your lungs and limiting your oxygen intake. But I'm damn thankful for its snug fit right now. Security blanket.

"Good luck."

I jump in.

I balance on the board. She pulls away, creating a wake. It's all I can do to stay sitting on top of the board.

Frankie waits a full minute before turning the lights on, continuing out to sea.

17

Pacific Ocean, CA

Photo: Boat, far away.

@georgeous A journey of a thousand miles begins with a single step. @laotsu

Destroying a criminal's boat begins with a single stroke. @georgeous

I slide my hand across the deck of Blake's board and into the water, pulling it back quietly. One stroke. The other side. Two. Repeat.

Frankie's been gone less than two minutes, and my heart rate has already hit 150/bpm. Do I know this because I have a waterproof Fitbit? No, but because I can feel my heartbeat in my throat.

Liam is pacing in the main part of the boat. On the phone. He looks irritated. Music? Blaring.

Paddle. Paddle. Paddle.

It's a clear night, but the open ocean is rough. As I get closer to the boat, Liam's pacing increases. It's a big boat. But there's not another soul on it. With a boat this big, you'd need another set of eyes to help you get it in and out of a slip or onto a trailer. At least a deck hand, if not two. Imagine parallel parking a G-Wagen in a spot meant for a motorcycle.

·

Paddle. Paddle. Paddle.

I feel like she dropped me off much closer than this.

A crank out another 50 strokes and get close.

Liam looks pissed.

He continues his pacing, while talking on the phone—pulling him back into the lower interior of the boat, out of sight.

I sprint.

Paddle. Paddle. Paddle.

Swell. Swell. Swell.

No wonder Frankie gave me fins. These swells are going to destroy the board. Nice of Blake to sacrifice it.

I paddle past the back of the boat and veer right. To the starboard side. It's a really nice boat. A mini yacht.

Resting my hand against the boat, it rocks with the swells.

Looking for something to grab onto, my eyes scan for one of those orange floating bumper thingies that make a million dollar boat look like a garbage wagon. But there are none. Just a single, elegant rubber strip, painted the same color as the hull. Maritime innovation and design has finally caught up with the Hyundai Elantra.

But the rubber strip is my friend. An easy-to-find grip line around the boat. Like a handrail in a dark movie theater.

•

A motorboat, unlike a car, has 99% of its guts toward the rear. Because the rudder is the two front tires. This may seem obvious, but it's not to me. Looking for where to anchor the surfboard, it's still counterintuitive to do it with the front 80% of the boat in front of me. Also, this places my hiding spot directly adjacent to Liam.

•

I palm my way along the rubber strip. Pushing up on it, I can reach up a few feet and grab the metal railing. Fortunately, Blake's surfboard has a nine-foot leash. Attaching it here, it'll either be conveniently tethered like my getaway horse or shredded into pieces.

I tie up the board, keeping the backpack on. My movements are cumbersome, with the glow sticks bracing my forearms.

I take the backpack off, balance it on the board and slide into the water next to it.

Dink. Dink. Dink.

I can already see the fiberglass cracking on Blake's board. Sorry brother.

A quick assessment.

Hmmm.

This is gonna be tricky.

I can use the fins to get a burst of power, if I need to get underneath the boat. But then I'm stuck cramming myself underneath the boat with fins on. Plus, nothing will be keeping the backpack afloat. The board is floaty, but it seems like it could shatter into debris at any moment.

I ponder being in the open ocean without fins. That decides it. I need to keep the fins with me at all times. Open ocean. No board. No land. Fins will at least give me a fighting chance.

Now the dikes or the hacksaw. Dikes are a no brainer. Relatively small, can tuck one handle into my wetsuit sleeve. Yes, next to a glow stick.

But the hacksaw is relatively foolproof; it doesn't require the force that the dikes will need, especially since I'll probably be in the water, with zero leverage. But the saw is almost impossible to swim with and could be loud.

Hmmm.

Dikes it is.

I slide the hacksaw back in the backpack and use the carabiner to clip the backpack to the railing of the boat. The surfboard will just have to stay tethered. It's the best option. I should have thought about all of this before. But at least the backpack isn't going anywhere.

Dikes in sleeve. Check.

Pulling fin #1 from the bag, the saw slips out. Hits the water.

Fuck.

Fumble. Fumble.

Grab. I catch it.

Jesus Fucking Christ.

As Liam cranks the volume on a fresh bro-rock tune, I swear I will wrap all of my tools in floating grip tape, for the rest of my life.

Fortunately, I did try the fins on beforehand, and they fit. I'm one for ten.

I tread water for a minute. Take in my surroundings.

I did not bring goggles.

Stupid.

I would make a terrible mercenary. The goggles wouldn't really be much use in the dark, but my eyes wouldn't be stinging from the salt water right now.

I reassess the boat.

I swim up and around the boat, to reassess. Confirmed—it is not the same boat from Frankie's diagram. Hers was for a *Chaparral*. The emblem on the side of the boat says: *Sea Wray*.

The different motors make sense.

Maya might have known this. Would she really not tell us that Frankie had the wrong blueprints? Or that we have the blueprints to their previous boat? It seems like too big of an oversight to not have been on purpose.

You can't exactly swap boats overnight. Wait, can you? It's hard to say. But she almost definitely knew that only Liam would be out here, by himself, or alerted Johnny to not be here. She threw us a bone with the map but protected her boyfriend.

•

Three laps around the boat.

Nothing.

Not one opening.

Not one accessible panel.

Nothing.

My only option: cut the fuel lines from the outboard motors. The only drawback: it's directly in Liam's line of sight. Also, it's directly in view of anyone looking to approach the boat and board it, because the entry steps are right next to the motors.

This is terrible.

•

I swim back to the board.

Think.

Hmmm.

"Ow!"

The side of the board I grab is splintered, from slamming into the hull. This board will be useless in five minutes. Sorry Blake.

I don't really have a choice.

I swim over, pull myself up onto the stoop next to an outboard motor and slide the dikes from my wetsuit sleeve. Pulling it from such tight quarters, it feels like half of my forearm skin might come with it.

The sliding door to the back of the boat opens. I duck.

Liam walks within a few feet of me, I presume to peer out over the open ocean. I can see the shadow of him waving his arms.

I look.

The other boat is on its way.

Fast.

"*Teenage. Mutant. Ninja. Turtles.*"

He walks back into the boat, and I stay crouched.

"What?"

...

"Why?"

...

"No..."

...

"Fuck! Fuck! Fuck!"

...

The other boat is coming in hot. Straight at me.

I slide into the water and kick hard. Diving deep under the boat and diagonally.

I pause for a second underneath the dead center of the boat. Making sure I'm not going to surface and be seen. Or get hurt.

Of the thousands of laps I've swam in my life, this is the moment that I savor most. The moment of total submersion. Even though I'm right in the middle of both witnessing and committing a crime, I'm under water. I am inside the earth. It's calming, given the current circumstances. I find it more meditative than any meditation. Is it baptism? Dying and coming to life again? I dunno. Returning to the womb? Probably. But, without a doubt, it is divine.

I slowly feel my way underneath the boat and surface.

Back to what's left of the surfboard.

I hear their motor. I'm lucky. They're coming from the other side. I'm completely shadowed. I can creep around the corner and watch their approach.

They are flying.

Their little boat does a quick whip turn and keeps the motor running.

It's Pretty Boy. And the girls. No Maya. No Johnny.

Liam's holding some rope, but Pretty Boy doesn't take it.

The girls look like they took a rollercoaster here—clinging on, hair matted from ocean spray.

Everything is not as planned.

They're yelling, but it's stifled by the rough water.

Pretty Boy ups the ante.

He yells, louder.

"No, no no!"

I think? Or maybe he yells:

"Go, go, go!"

He drops the hammer on the boat and does a water burnout.

They're gone.

Oh, man.

What should I do?

All I can think of is Maya. What did she actually say to Johnny?

Doesn't matter. I've gotta be quick.

Liam strolls into the interior of the boat.

I dive back under.

Feel my way underneath the boat.

Thank god it's new and not covered in barnacles.

I grab the back landing platform, with my left hand—the one that's not holding the dikes.

Pull myself up.

Look for Liam.

He's inside. Back on the phone.

I slide the head of the dikes over the fuel line and wince at the upcoming onslaught of fuel that's going to spray on me and drip into the water.

Environmentally, this plan is terrible.

Grip.

Grip.

Adding extra strength by silently grunting…

Nothing.

The fuel lines are too thick.

I try both hands.

Nope.

"Fuck." I only mouth it. But it feels like a scream.

I drop the dikes.

Ding.

I catch them but only after they've hit the metal bracing bar. Metal on metal sounds aren't always the quietest.

I hear a muffled expletive almost instantly.

"What the fuck?" Liam stomps back through the open doors.

I dive, dive and kick, keeping my arms behind me, dikes firmly gripped in my right hand.

I swim back diagonally underneath the boat. I reach the board. Or what's left of it. The top half of the board has broken off. What remains is getting battered against the hull like a three-foot saltine. The backpack, weighed down with flares and the hacksaw, without the fins as floatation, is thankfully still clipped to the boat's railing.

Keeping my eyes alert for Liam possibly walking the boat's

perimeter, I unclip the backpack.

I unzip it, slide the dikes in and cinch it tight. Pulling it over my shoulders and clipping the chest strap, I kick with the fins a few times. Seeing if swimming with it on my back is doable. It is.

"*Teenage. Mutant. Ninja. Turtles…*" It really is a catchy tune. High five, Nickelodeon. For such a piece of shit, Liam does have some interesting layers.

His phone blowing up is my good fortune. Distraction. Inability to follow up on disconcerting sounds coming from the wide-open, empty ocean.

•

Back to the motors. My heart rate has settled at a medium-intense 120/bpm. Still freaked out by almost getting caught by Liam, I've let go of trying to fully calm myself.

One other thing I should have brought? A waterproof flashlight. The flares are waterproof but not once lit. Plus, they're extremely unstealth, dangerous and impractical for subtler applications. Such as finding a fuel line to cut. The glowsticks would work, but they're my only life-line back to Frankie. I wish I could settle for cutting the wire chassis of crucial electrical wires, but fear of electrocution makes this imprudent.

•

Pop up on the stoop; slide back in the water; repeat. Not super easy, with the dikes in my right hand. I can't find anything I can cut, without killing myself. This motor is just too well made. Thanks a lot, Yamaha.

Gawah.

Gawah.

Gawawawahrooom.

Liam starts the motor. A change to the sex-at-sea plan.

I grab onto the back, hitching a ride. It's reminiscent of being a kid, skateboarding up to a Winnebago and grabbing the ladder to sneak a lift.

This is a disaster. If Liam takes us even two minutes in any direction, Frankie will never find me.

"*Teenage. Mutant. Ninja. Turtles…*"

"What? I'm coming!" He keeps the phone at his ear and accelerates. It's too much. I won't be able to hang on. I've got to get in the boat.

I slide over the back edge. Because I still have the fins on, I have to semi-stand and can't hide.

Mistake.

Liam's got the backdoor open, and I watch him at the controls. My feet are staggered. I squat half yoga/half kung fu, but stability escapes me. He hangs up his phone. I freeze.

He slams the throttle.

Hard.

I topple instantly.

Thud. Thud. Thud.

Liam spins around. Shocked.

Scared, for a millisecond. But that millisecond passes, when he sees that it's me. With impressive fluidity, he glances ahead of us and kills the throttle.

Then?

He leaps. Lunges really. Toward me.

I'm three long strides away. By step number two, he's got his arm cocked back with a haymaker.

On my back, the fins are straight up, creating a two-foot rubber barrier between us.

"YOU.MOTHER.FU…"

I'm impressed by his fight or flight instinct. He goes from distracted to annoyed to action in a blink.

He jumps. Clears the fins. Unleashes his punch.

Repetition. Practice. It works. It turns voluntary actions that require will and thought into involuntary actions. Actions that can't be undone.

His punch starts from behind his shoulder, but my arms are already up, in defense.

The dikes. In my fist. I'm not trying to make it happen. I'm witnessing it. As if I'm six inches away from myself. Or six miles.

By the time Liam's punch breaks the plane of his other shoulder, my fist connects with his throat. Not even that hard. But it's backed with the steel ruthlessness of the dikes. Just a thunk of his Adam's apple. It's enough.

Feeling his skin, I instinctively pivot. From prey to predator. From defense to offense. I let him fall—half on me, half on the boat.

Ghuh.

It sounds like Rocky hitting the side of beef.

"Uouchghoochghhh!"

The sound of him choking on his own throat? Music to my fucking ears. Strain. The only other sound is the boat motors, chugging away.

Galug. Galug. Galug.

"Cah Cak Cah."

Liam sounds like he's breathing through a clogged Circle K coffee stirrer. He grabs me.

For help? To hurt me?

I pivot. Twist. Sit on top of him. The fins don't allow me to do it gracefully, and it forces my knees against his shoulders. Once I settle, settle into using him as a chair, it's comfortable. Natural to sit on him.

Liam is completely immobilized. No longer a threat.

I look down at him in disgust.

"You worthless piece of shit."

His eyes get wide. Scared? Angry? Both? I have no idea. But the primary feeling that I feel? Mad. Super mad.

"Ooohn't!"

"Did you just say, 'don't'?"

Again, I leave my body. But this time closer. Just an inch or two away. I flip the dikes in my hand. Catching them like a playful electrician.

Cock back and...

18

I remember my high school biology teacher saying the words *vitreous humor*. Even the two words together sound disgusting. But putting a scalpel into a cow's eye? It wasn't the fetid Jell-O that made me gag, it was the horrific sound of penetrating the eye.

Biology dissection lab. That's what comes to mind, as my arms hover over Liam, about to blind him, briefly, before shoving the dikes into his skull.

Spectator. Passenger. Driver. I realize even being open to the opportunity of killing Liam and Johnny was absurd. I still doubt they are redeemable. But I think of Liam surfing. A horrible person doing something beautiful. And that's why we don't murder. That's why have due process. Because, even if some people can't heal or grow, we have to create a world where they could. Where even for a villain, there is hope.

I've been so adamant about being the driver, I didn't fully internalize what that meant. I thought driver was synonymous with unilateral decision making.

It's not.

•

"Uhhh huuuh Uhhh huuuh" Liam is catching his breath. Barely. He can see I've lost my death glare, and it's calmed him. He has hope.

If I'm not going to kill him, I can't allow him to fully recover. To become a threat again. I remember him kicking me, three on one. While he was on the phone. It makes my blood boil.

He feels my body go rigid. Resolute. His fear returns.

"Ohn ohn ohn!" A compromised version of *no no no.*

Yes yes yes.

I look at the dikes. They're still nose down in my hand. I lean harder on his chest.

"Uhhht!" Liam returns to gasping. The lack of oxygen during the last few minutes has left him weak. I pin his arm down at the wrist. He balls his fist, in defiance, but it's useless.

Have you ever ground pepper with a pestle? Crushed medication with a prescription bottle for your grandma?

"Aaahhh ohn!!!!"

"*Teenage! Mutant! Ninja! Turtles!* Don't worry Liam! I'll sing to you!"

Slowly, I hammer Liam's hand and wrist. About seven or eight times. Some blood. But not much.

The broken bones make his hand look like chicken skin pulled over a bag of candy corn.

"Ahhh!"

"Swear you will never touch a zip tie, as long as you live. Or I'll break your other hand, too."

I pump-fake grabbing his other hand.

"Ooohhhnnn!!!"

•

The motors. I've gotta stop the boat. Otherwise, it'll idle us too far away from Frankie.

I stand, again forgetting that I have the fins on.

"Jesus."

Knowing that the most fucked up moment of the night is over (hopefully), my heartbeat slows. But my gut churns. I don't foresee a future career as an enforcer.

Plus, the sound of Liam's whimpering is annoying.

There was only a small spattering of blood. I pull off the fins and dip my hands into the ocean. I wipe them on a clean part of Liam's shirt. It's discourteous but very effective.

"Ahh!" A small protest, from a very compromised man.

Does he know I want to break his feet, too?

I walk into the boat, see one of his hoodies and use it as a glove. No fingerprints. No blood smears. Just wet feet. On a boat. No biggie. I'm not sure that my fingerprints will matter, but better safe than sorry.

I kill the motor. You'd think it'd be more complicated, but it's not. A keychain dangles, and a quarter turn of the ignition key kills it.

My eyes land on Liam's radio.

Hmmm.

•

A bit of pacing. It feels like an eternity. The thought of swimming a few miles to shore sounds terrible. Terrible. I could do it. It'd take forever, but with fins, it's do-able.

Let's see. Say we're now three miles out. With currents, waves, all in, let's double that and call it six miles. At two miles an hour, it'd take me three hours. I'll be cold, and starving, but I'll be alive. And home. Unless I get spotted by the Coast Guard or a great white.

My eyes re-find the radio.

Hmmm.

And what to do with Liam?

•

Being dumbfounded continues for a few more seconds. I snap on the radio and listen to our channel. Nothing.

Nothing. Nothing. Nothing.

I look at Liam. Shivering. In pain. Obedient.

Then? A crackle comes from the radio.

"Anaconda, come in."

"Hail me a Crab! The sails are gone! Long gone! No more sailing tonight! Got it?"

Raj, excited, panicked, over-communicates.

"Copy." Frankie—the consummate professional.

"Sorry! I mean over!"

I can't resist. A risk I probably shouldn't take—advertising my voice on a hostile vessel. I grab the radio. It's either the smartest or the dumbest thing I will ever do.

"Possible motor trouble on Rendezvous at Sea. Significant drifting. Be alert. Over."

"Roger. Over and out." Frankie takes the minimal information and severs our conversation. She's the most level-headed all of us. She heard my anxiety. Heard my message. *You're gonna have to look a bit harder. But come. Come find me. Come now.*

•

"What are you gonna do, man?!"

Liam is slowly gaining his voice. Disappointing progress. He's also standing. Almost. He's cowering so severely, it's hard to believe he's upright.

"Shut up. I'm gonna save your life. But if you say fucking boo, I'm gonna hurt you. I mean really hurt you. Do you understand? Let me put this life vest on you." He acquiesces. He's got no other choice.

It's one of those over-the-neck life vests, and I consider using the nylon strap to pin his arms to his sides. But it's not necessary. His resistance is zero. He's used to being told what to do.

I look around the boat. The boat bought with proceeds from human trafficking. How soon will tonight be forgotten and another three women be tortured on this thing?

How about never.

I break the glow sticks and set them on the fins, next to Liam. He looks like an overgrown child in the life vest. I wish I had enough time to shave off that sparse moustache.

I turn the key.

Gawah.

Gawah.

Gawawawahrooom.

What a waste of such a beautiful boat. I hit the throttle and gently turn the boat around. Point it due west. Out to sea.

Galuglugluglug.

It moves slowly. Resolutely. Like a tank on a backcountry road.

I walk into the kitchen. Turn on the gas on the two stove burners. The scent is intoxicating, like a strong inhale at the gas pump. Delicious. Volatile.

But I don't ignite them.

The flares.

•

"Ahhh!"

Splash.

Liam in the water. Done.

Then, I light both the flares over the water. If you've never ignited a flare, it's 5% thrilling and 95% absolutely terrifying. They didn't design them to look like sticks of dynamite by accident.

I left Liam's mostly dry hoodie across the track of the sliding glass door. A bridge from inside to out. Even a bit blood-soggy, it'll be a perfect fuse.

•

Another twenty seconds.

I'm at the edge of the boat, about to jump. I see Frankie. Thank god. I wave the flares. Maybe ten times. She flicks the lights, quickly. Three times. Not over-bright. But enough to let me know. I love her.

Flare #1.

I drop it in a cup holder next to the sliding glass door. It rests against Liam's vape pen and cannabis oil. Unfortunate collateral damage.

The flares will burn for fifteen minutes. It's my backup plan, but I can't help but wince, expecting an explosion. Nothing. Not yet.

Flare #2. I set on top of Liam's damp hoodie. The carpet next to it singes instantly, and, after a moment, one of the hood strings lights. It may not be as damp as I thought. Time to get out of here.

Fins. Glow sticks. Both of my hands are full. I jump in the water, treading away from the boat. A convenient spot for the glow sticks is absent. I give up, sliding them back down my sleeves. So I can get the fins on. So I can make some distance away from the massive floating bomb.

I grab onto Liam's bobbing body. His face is ghostlike from the cold water and lack of circulation.

"Liam, you don't look good. A bit like DiCaprio's last scene in *The Titanic.*"

He doesn't reply.

•

Galugluglug.

Even at idle, the boat moves quick. Quick enough that I'd have to swim hard to keep up with it.

In moments, it's gone. The silence and darkness of the open ocean greet us.

"We're gonna drown out here!"

"No, we're not. At least I'm not. And shut the fuck up."

My own adrenalin fades, and the cold replaces it. The cold has been there all night. But now I really notice it, even in the wetsuit. Liam must be freezing. I turn, looking for Frankie. But now that I'm in the water, my vision is obscured by the swells. All I can see is Liam's boat, slowly fading. Diminishing.

Kick. Kick. Crest wave. Look.

Kick. Kick. Crest wave. Look.

Liam has simmered down. Accepted whatever fate has in store for him. Accepted being dragged by the collar, like a disobedient dog. Guess who's not here to help, bro? Johnny.

I'm starting to get a little scared. I feel like I'm on Apollo 13 and Houston is a million miles away. But as soon as there's panic, there's hope.

A swell picks me up, and I see Frankie's boat cross Liam's. Frankie has kept her distance, but I can almost feel her turn her head. Studying it as it passes. Curious. Understanding.

I'm starting to question whether Frankie still sees me, or if she's just chugging straight towards home. I, too, head toward shore, by kicking on my back. Pacing her. Waving the glow sticks every twenty seconds or so. Dragging the dead weight of shivering Liam with me.

I saved his life. Kind of. And now I'm going to kill him, accidentally, with hypothermia.

•

Frankie's flashlight hits me with a flicker of light. She sees me. The position of the boat leans back, rising up in the swells. She's accelerating.

Phew.

•

In the distance—fire. A big fire.

"George!"

"Hey!" My teeth chatter.

"Here! Grab!"

She reaches out with her own life jacket, using it for the extra reach. She must've kept it handy as a backup plan. Seriously, this one does not miss a beat.

"You brought this fucking piece of shit with you?"

"I know. I surprise even myself at times. Let's pull him in. He's halfway to freezing to death."

"Good." But she grabs his shoulder.

"Huhgh." We grunt. "Liam. Fuck. Push with your legs or something. Christ."

He gives a lackluster leg hook onto the boat, but it's enough.

"Jesus. Look at his fingers…oh my god!"

"Just get him a blanket. Anything. Me too."

•

"Did you see? The boat? I saw you cross it."

"You mean what's left of it? Look."

She hands me the mini binoculars. I grab it with one hand and take off a fin with the other. I'm so happy to be out of the water; I forget that I'm cold for a second.

"Oh my god." Liam's boat is a floating, raging inferno.

"Yeah. When I passed it? The cabin was lit up like a bonfire. Twenty seconds later? Kaboom."

"Damn."

"What happened?"

"I'll tell you later. I presume you saw the other boat? With the passengers? Using this thingie?"

"Monocular. For someone who lives for word choice, you're sure struggling with this one."

"Did you see…"

"I did." She looks at Liam. "You're right. Let's talk about it later."

19

"Do you think Blake'll mind if I wear this?"

"Nope."

I've got my own clothes on, but I'm still freezing. I snagged one of Blake's jackets, and my monkey arms hang out of it.

"I won't even ask about his surfboard."

"Hopefully he gets a discount at 2 Mile Surf Shop?"

She's laser focused on driving. I give her a side hug. We both look at Liam on the deck, broken. Fetal.

"Frankie, you're a sight for sore eyes."

"You too."

My adrenalin is dropping. And so is my energy.

"George?"

"Yeah?"

"Two more things?"

"OK."

"Grab us a beer. And put your hands on that fish." She jerks her head toward two coolers. A beer one and a fish one. Both Yetis, and I'm pleased. It has been established that I am a brand loyalist.

"Perfect. I'm so thirsty."

"You can drink both. Just leave a few sips in mine. As a decoy. And then put your hands on the fish."

"Gross, why?"

"Because we just caught them. An outdoorsy couple. Out night fishing. Couple of brews. Relatively wholesome. It's not foolproof, but it's better than nothing."

"Halibut?"

"Yep?"

"You caught these fish?"

"Yeah. From a guy at the dock. This afternoon, idiot."

"Ohhh." I crack the beers and admire our daily limit catch. "Frankie, you are so on top of it, so organized. The Container Store would make you their CEO. Always two steps ahead."

"I anticipated everything except you bringing this fool onboard. Nobody's on a fishing trip, with hands like that."

"We saved him. From that pesky electrical fire."

"Wow, we're really nice."

•

It's not a long boat ride, but I'm asleep with my eyes wide open, by the time we hit the dock in Bolinas.

•

"Why don't you hop out? Take this bag of nothingness with you. I've gotta head to the marina. Pick you up at Smiley's?"

"Yeah, yeah."

"You sure? You look a little comatose."

"Nah, I'll snap out of it."

"Go get a drink. Your shift is over. But hand me Liam's lifejacket. It's not a good look."

"Oh, right."

•

Liam, sprung from the life vest, attempts to sprint off. But he's too beat down. And cold. It's a slow-motion sprint.

I grab him and pin him to the dock post. Cock my fist at the ready. Again, he does not resist.

"Aaagh. Please man. Please."

I pull one of his hands behind his back—the broken one.

"Ahhhgh! Come on, man!"

"You're gonna get in that beater Ford Ranger. And you're gonna drive. You will never return here. And if you so much as wave at Johnny, I'm going to find you, and I'm going to hurt you. Do you understand?" How will I follow through on this threat? I have no idea. All that Liam knows is that I was able to find him on the open sea. And that's all that matters.

"OK, man! OK!"

"The only reason I'm not taking you to jail right now is because I'm afraid they'd let you go. I'm going to beg the girls to testify. So here's your one chance. Go."

•

I walk the short distance to Smiley's.

A familiar Tacoma is parked in front.

The passenger is even more familiar.

Maya's alone. The window is down.

She looks very put-together, other than her eyes looking like a teary raccoon's.

"You didn't tell me we planned for the wrong boat. That almost got me fucking killed, Maya."

She looks straight ahead, with quick glances at me.

Johnny must be nearby.

"Where are the girls?"

"At home. Our home. They're fine. Raj is there. All of them are safe."

"All but one."

She looks in the rearview mirror, quickly. Johnny must be at the Bolinas People's Store.

"George. Go. Please. Just go."

"Get out of the truck. Come with me. It's over."

"I can't. I love him."

"Maya, his boat is a floating barbeque. That will not go unnoticed. Even if you flee to some lawless Humboldt outpost, Johnny will eventually get found. There will be questions. And he won't have answers. Maya, come on…"

Bang.

Not a gunshot. A door slam. I look. There he is.

He saunters out, carrying a bag of groceries with two Duraflame logs sticking out.

"Professor. You look like yah've been rode hard and put away wet. Musta had a busy night."

"Going camping?"

He puts the bag down in the middle of the street. Pulls out the Duraflame logs. They're $15 apiece at the store. For emergency camping trips only.

We both square off to fight.

But both of us are hesitant.

If one of those Duraflames connects with my head, I'm not gonna get back up. And I already want to lie down.

Johnny knows that even wasting thirty extra seconds on me is a mistake. And he certainly doesn't need to add an assault charge to what might be assembled over the next few weeks.

A standoff.

I break it.

"If anything happens to Maya. Anything…"

Thud. Thud.

He responds by throwing the groceries and logs into the back of the truck.

"You take care now, Professor."

The truck starts flawlessly, like every Toyota.

He reverses quickly, without looking, nearly hitting me.

They kick up a little dust.

But not enough to obscure the letters on his license plate.

•

For once in my life, I'm not in the mood to be in a bar. I wait outside for Frankie, and she pulls up in her truck like she expected me to.

I hop in. Energy fading. Repeating the sequence over and over.

"Do you have a pen?"

"Yeah."

She grabs one from the visor.

"2XU…"

She stops writing.

"I know Johnny's license plate too, dumbass."

"Of course you do."

Yawn. I'm trying to get the last tête-à-tête with Johnny out of my mouth, but my whole body is starting to shut down.

"Big night, eh?"

"That was a long twenty minutes. I'm exhausted."

She kisses me.

And lingers.

It's wonderful.

"The girls are at home."

"Really?"

"Yeah. With Raj. Johnny and Maya just took off."

"Fuck."

"I tried."

"To get him? To grab her?"

"Both."

•

We walk in, feeling the heat of multiple bodies but almost no sound.

The door to Maya's room: open. Her room: empty. Empty in the dump all of your clothes on your bed and roll your whole life into a duvet-burrito kind of empty. It's not looking good for her cleaning deposit. The cats? They're either with her or have relocated. This last note does not break my heart. Note: cats are cool and survivalistic. Just occasionally lack good timing.

"Fuuuck."

"Yeah."

Frankie tugs my hand. Pulls me into the family room.

"Hi guys!" Raj turns to the girls. "This is Frankie and George. Her boyfriend." He turns to one of them "Mes amis utiles."

Boyfriend. Hearing him say this, it sounds forced. But when you're trying to pacify three trafficked women, you'll do anything to calm them. Well played Raj.

Plus, I kinda like it.

Bolinas, CA—The Farm
Photo: Three stoic, trafficked women sitting on the floor in a house whose biggest previous crime was serving a meal without kale.
@georgeous I can see Russia from my house. @sarahpalin

Damn, anxiety makes my social media jokes dark.

"Raj. I didn't know you could braid hair?" But I could have

guessed.

"It's all in the wrist!"

It's comforting to know he was here with them.

They introduce themselves.

"Olga."

"Khulan."

"Tatiana."

I'm charmed by their grace and decorum.

My fatigue hits, and all I hear is something that sounds like Stoli.

•

Shower. Heaven.

I ignore the decades-long California drought and shower until I'm fully warm. 20 minutes? It feels like two sighs and a blink. I hear Raj exit the house, and Frankie heel-walks towards the bathroom. She walks loud.

"Can I come in?"

"Of course."

She walks in.

"Oh. I thought you were bringing me a beer."

"It's not that kind of night, George."

She pulls a nylon re-usable bag from her pocket. She grabs a high-end electric toothbrush, organic mouthwash and large brandless bottle of lotion.

"Just the essentials?"

"Yep."

"I love that lotion on you. It smells like macaroons."

"A woman makes it by hand in Point Reyes. Can't risk leaving it."

"You know, we're not outlaws. At least not yet."

"Better safe than sorry."

"Fair."

She kisses my chest.

"Since Raj called you my boyfriend, which was super fucking cute by the way, I will bring you a beer. But in bed. Let's go to bed."

"What about the…?"

"I gave them blankets. They're sharing the couches. They want to stay together."

"Ah. Right." I look at my watch. "Hey. Did Raj see Maya earlier?"

"Yeah." She takes on a Raj posture. A tinge more feminine than her own. "I came here to wait for you two. By the way, I love those succulents you have in the kitchen window. Anyway, Maya came in and dropped them off! I'd never seen her in makeup! It looked ah-mazing! She should do that more often!"

"You're way too good at that."

"Right? Anyway, as soon as they got home, she grabbed all her shit and rolled." Frankie eyes a nearly-new thing of floss and throws it in her bag.

"So, beer? Yes?"

"Stronger."

"You want to say vodka, don't you? But you're afraid it's inappropriate? Because it fucking is, George."

"Uhhh…"

She shakes her head and walks out.

•

"Sorry. All we had for mixer was Orangina."

I grab it and take a swig.

"Delicious." I nearly finish it.

"Um, we were sharing that."

"Doh."

She finishes the dregs.

"Wow. This really is good."

•

Three sex trafficked refugees on the couch, and I'm having a: *How was your day?* conversation with my girlfriend of two days. What could go wrong?

"Here!" She made two more. I can tell that they're stronger, because the Orangina color is faint at the top, with a vodka floater.

"How do you feel about the phrase 'that's my girl'? Because it's been on repeat in my head."

"I think you're a fucking idiot. But it's not without its charms. Continue."

We drink. Share half smiles. She can see how tired my eyes are. I've got about two minutes left in me. Not much time left for her to strike. But one of women's many superpowers is skillfully sneaking in just one more question. Just one.

She wants to know everything. But she lets it go. And takes my glass.

In a few blinks, I feel her hands on me.

Then, blackness.

•

I sleep for a few hours. Not long enough. Then I wake from an invisible nightmare. Or wake up to one. Thinking of everything that needs to be done. To keep us all safe. To keep all of us from getting caught.

Mainly, that I'm about to drive hundreds of miles in my van, with four women and not enough seatbelts. Getting pulled over might result in questions I don't want to answer and three passports we can't provide.

I can feel that Frankie isn't asleep. But she's letting me wake up on my own. Not pushing it.

"Frankie. We need to go. We can't stay here."

"We need to wait. Just a few more hours."

I look at the clock. 3:30am.

"I dunno."

"At least until 6:30. Then we can just be part of the sea of commuters heading south into the city. Way less conspicuous."

"OK. OK. That makes sense." I look at the clock again. "Fuck. That feels like forever." I settle back into bed. Restless. She can feel it.

She waits about two minutes. But I'm already ready.

"Sooo, Liam?"

"Plausible deniability?"

"I drove the fucking boat, George. I'm a full-fledged accomplice. Oh, also? I have three gorgeous Russian girls with no passports in my living room."

"One of them is from the Ukraine and the other Mongolia. And you miscounted. There are four gorgeous women in this house."

"I'm not that easy."

"Didn't say you were."

"Grrr."

I kiss her. She kisses me back. Hard. But then she stops.

"Spill it."

"I went for the outboards. Liam heard me. And saw me. Attacked me."

"Oh my god."

"I got the upper hand. And I did consider killing him. Or leaving him behind, on the boat. But I couldn't do it. I was so, so tempted. But I couldn't." I stare at her. "Honestly, Frankie. It felt natural. Right. Simple. Like checking out of a grocery store. But instead of being handed a receipt I was going to stick the dikes through his eyeball into his brain."

"Gross." She cringes. I'm not sure if it's because of the visual or my ambivalence towards it.

"But it just felt like I was perpetuating something bad. You know? I'm not a murderer."

"So you mangled his hand? That's less violent? That's almost worse."

20

"How long? Is dee drivink?"

"Uh, maybe two hours? Longer if we're stuck in this traffic the whole way. Can you guys get a little lower? I'm sorry, we just really don't want to…"

Tatiana turns to her squad.

"Nizhe." All of them melt into the floor, without a murmur. The Mongolian woman (again, it feels absurd to call her that, she is so, so young), Khulan, is completely invisible, underneath my surfboard.

Frankie grabs my hand. Kisses it. Then lets it go. So, I can return it to the steering wheel.

"You're awfully sweet lately."

"Hey sugar? Keep your eyes on the fucking road."

•

I can hear them whispering. But it's faint. Respectful. They're scared out of their minds, and their deference humbles me.

•

We hit Gilroy. The land where garlic begins and where the Bay Area ends into farmland and rolling hills. Maiming a piece of human garbage and blowing up a boat feels far, far away.

"George, slow down please."

I look. 80mph.

"Sorry. Spaced."

"You good? Want me to drive?"

"I'm good. But feel free to rub my forearm."

•

Every time I listen to the silence of our passengers, I'm stunned by their acceptance. Accepting of the plot of a movie they never got to preview.

Frankie breaks through my trance.

"This place. In Monterey. Are you sure? Seems vague. Sketchy or something."

"I'm sure."

•

We get there.

Well, we get close.

Four U turns.

I focus. Frankie gets concerned. Our passengers? Unflappable. What will happen will happen.

Their resolve depresses and enlightens me. And I pray I never have to learn to live how they do.

"Der." Tatiana's head pops up like a meerkat. She points her finger. "There?"

"Yes."

"How do you know the address?"

"Do not. That one. Lockbox."

I pull in the driveway. A completely innocuous suburban house, with fresh paint.

A four number combination lock, hanging from the front door handle. I visualize a numeric keypad. Then give up and pull out my phone. S…I…F…U , 8…4…6…3

Pull. Nothing.

Pull. Nothing.

Check numbers. Correct.

Pull.

Click.

Olga, who has not uttered a single sound on this entire journey, sighs in relief. Tatiana follows with four quiet, firm words. She changes from sentry to communicator and back to sentry in a moment. I don't speak Russian, but I understand her gist: *One more night, we will survive.*

•

A simple, stucco house. Nothing covering the concrete floors in the living room and kitchen, but the two bedrooms are immaculate and full of furniture.

My eyes take a quick inventory. Thermostat. Blankets. Canned goods. Some basics. Pasta.

Tatiana picks it up. Switching our roles. Another handful of words and all three are in motion. Boiling water. Making beds. It's like watching Delta Force clear a house.

I fiddle with the thermostat. Tatiana gives me a flat palm to stop.

"Long drivink. And tomorrow. Take the restink. We make tea. Some food."

"OK. Thank you."

She creases her eyes in an almost smile.

•

I sip the tea and lean back on the bed. The tea tastes incredible, and I'm not even sick. Being here feels like a teleportation of last night— two in one room, three in another.

Frankie is cleaning up next to me with some baby wipes. She was smart to bring them. I should do the same. I watch her wipe underneath her shirt. I want to touch her.

Where are we all going to sleep?

But then?

Sleep.

•

"Uh, uh. Sorry. I crashed. What's up?"

"We're good. Go back to sleep." She kisses my forehead. "Wait. Listen."

I do.

The three of them are chatting in the other room. Quietly. But it's clearly a story. And a nice one. Some small laughter.

"I've never actually heard the sound of hope. So sweet."

"Yeah. They're so inspiring. And you need to stop calling them girls."

"You're right."

•

"You sure?"

"Yep."

"No note, nothing?"

"Nope. We're good. Sergeant Tatiana's contribution of cleaning this place into oblivion is more than enough."

"But we should at least leave a bottle of wine?"

"Frankie. Sometimes, we have to just accept favors."

•

The ladies are already in the van. Their somberness is back. We're five hours from LA. There are consulates for all three countries in San Francisco, but we all agreed getting some distance between us and the nearby ears of Bolinas was the best move. For all five of us.

Frankie locks up. Scrambling the combo. Her competence at life makes her my number one draft pick. She was tied with Blake. But now that we're sleeping together, I have to support nepotism. I would love to meet Blake's wife, though. He clearly has excellent taste in women.

"Who gave you this place?"

"My Si…my…a friend."

"That's a good friend."

"Yeah." I want to say that he is and was more than a friend. But I can't think of how to explain it. What's more is I really don't want to. She can see me taking a moment, as I turn right. Away from the driveway. Away from Sifu Mark's gift of a safe haven. Frankie suppresses her untiring curiosity to let me have this one. For myself.

Someday, if we're still together, I'll tell her about him. About how he taught me how to be like water, in his goofy, hairy-eared dad kinda way.

•

An hour outside of LA, Tatiana, Khulan and Olga are huddled together in the back of the van. They've become like a group of sisters on vacation. But these ones never ask: *Are we there yet?* Because their there, by every measure, is so far away.

"Hello? Sure, I'll hold."

…

Frankie looks at me, impatiently. I nod my head. Supporting her but also telling her to chill.

"Yes, yes! I'm here. We have a really unique situation…"

CAST, the Coalition to Abolish Slavery and Trafficking, is headquartered off Wilshire in LA. This was Frankie's brainchild. I didn't really have a plan, other than LAPD and my mom's house. LAPD sees so much trafficking, they could at least point us in the right direction. And my mom is great at cooking for groups. I'd love to see her fight for alpha female status with Tatiana. Or Frankie, for that matter.

"No, their passports were taken…"

…

"I'd rather not say. We're a bit compromised."

…

"When? Oh, today. Is that possible? We'd be there before 3."

...

"Three. One Russian, one Ukrainian and one Mongolian."

...

"Ha. Yes. Of course. They are safe. Sorry to laugh. It just…it took a lot to…"

...

"Thank you. That means a lot."

...

She sighs.

"No police report. That I know of. That was part of the problem."

...

"No, I uh…Can this be anonymous?"

...

"OK. Well, one of the previous women did contact the Sheriff's Department. In Marin County."

...

"Sure, I just…OK. Yeah, I'll hold."

She looks at me. I have a million questions, but I don't want to jeopardize the conversation.

...

"I'm here. I'm here."

...

"Yes. Marin County."

...

"Really? No way. Wow."

...

"No, I just…it's a place stuck in time. You'd never think anyone would talk. But that's good to know. Thank you."

…

"Well, we're on our way. I can't thank you enough. My name's Frankie, by the way."

…

"Wonderful to meet you Alexandra. Again, we can't thank you enough."

…

"Ha! Thank you! You too!"

She hangs up.

"Are you guys starting a book club, or what?"

"She's so cool. Got everything instantly. They're a bit bootstrapped, but they can kick off the documentation. Get the passports going. She said she'd look into local shelter availability, but she needs to talk to them each in person, before they can place them somewhere. It's good we have your mom's house as a backup. It's not perfect, but it's something."

"Marin County Sheriff?"

"Yeah, right? After the APB Raj sent out, one of the sheriff guys got spooked. Spilled. That's all she had. But it sounds like legit officials are looking into it."

"That is a miracle. Can we also absolutely-not-anonymously leave Johnny's license plate number?"

"I'm sure they can figure it out. Plus, I left it with Raj last night, you were in the shower, smarty-pants."

•

Frankie grabs my arm. I don't know what happened, other than us pulling off a pretty epic crime, but she is a different person toward me.

"So, after this. San Luis Obispo. Are you still down?"

"One hundred percent."

"George. It's OK, if you're not. If it's too much."

"I'm down. OK? Plus, you're stuck with me for at least a few days right now. And there's a strong possibility you will meet my mother tonight. If it's not too much." I love using people's words back against them.

"Oh god."

She smiles, then turns. Looks back at the girls. They're deep in a very quiet conversation—something personal and positive. The Mongolian girl, err woman, either understands a bit of Russian or, like everyone else on earth, understands tonality. You can see it in her reactions. Because when we talk about love and relationships, it always sounds the same. It's the story of humanity.

"George."

She looks at me. Straight in the eyes. She breaks her stare, giving me my eyes back to the road. She looks out over the ocean. I check the road. It's wide open, and I follow her eyes. Is she checking the surf? It actually looks pretty good. Clean. Shoulder high.

"What's up, Frankie?"

"Thank you."

"I've been meaning to say the exact same thing to you."

•

Carpentaria. Ventura. Camarillo. The ocean disappears into a sea of freeways. LA. I glance at my passengers in the rearview. Everyone is sleepy from the long drive. Including me.

Maybe some sugar.

•

We're sitting in a Walmart parking lot, in the massive parking lot that is Los Angeles.

I bought Tatiana a burner phone. Just in case.

Frankie is programming our two numbers into it.

I split up a monster Kit Kat.

Frankie looks up.

"You really love those things, eh?"

"I love the texture. I was trying to break the habit, to avoid early onset diabetes, but now they make them in dark chocolate. I surrender."

"Surrender me another piece."

I do.

"OK. For processed food, it's pretty good. You're onto something with the texture."

"It's also not humanly possible to walk into Walmart and only come out with a phone. All of those bright colors and 88 cent signs. It's gross. But it works. Marketing."

The girls smile. I doubt they understand my odd humor, but they can witness that all of our moods have lifted.

I turn to Tatiana.

"Tatiana, this phone is just in case, OK? We'll drop you off. Get you checked in, so they can work on your passports and stuff. Then come back in a few hours. I promise."

"OK. Dis coming back. Is no need. We are OK."

"We're coming back. Even if they find you a shelter, I think all three of you should stay with me at my mom's for a day or two, at least. OK?"

"Actually, I will stay with you, Tatiana." Frankie pipes up. She looks at me. "It just seems smarter, right? It's only for a few hours. I mean you will come back, right George?" She smirks.

"Yeah. It's a great call. Plus, I can soften the blow with my mom, about her having four new roommates."

•

Standing outside of CAST, it feels more respectful to give Frankie a kiss on the forehead and big hug. Versus the intense kissing we've been getting a lot of practice at the last few days.

"See you in a few hours?"

"Yep. I mean, I kinda wanna bail, but you did pick me up out at sea. So, I owe you a solid."

"You're such a fucker."

•

"Hi sweetheart!"

"Hi mom."

She glances at Frankie's bag, registering that it is clearly not mine, and doesn't say a word.

"You're back! I'm so glad you're safe." She gives me a hug. "Let me guess, something happened and you are taking off tomorrow."

"Uhhh, actually, I wanted to stay for a bit, but was gonna ask if I could bring some guests?"

"Guests? As in more than one?"

"Well, primarily one, but…"

"That was fast."

"What was fast? The trip or…"

She smirks.

The same way I do, when I like my own joke.

Reminding me that I'm home.

•••

Acknowledgments

For the many years I've lived in San Francisco, Bolinas has been a welcome haven and reprieve. Don't believe the hype—Bolinas is quite welcome to outsiders, especially if you respect it a fraction of how much its inhabitants love it. Bolinas is a special place.

My apologies to Marin County Law Enforcement for being cast as villains. It's fiction; I swear.

My editor, Jennifer Lewis is a delight, brilliant and fun to trade with.

Pilar Alessandra, my writing coach, is my friend as much as she is my guide.

Maddy Hutchison is simply the best and has been, throughout this entire series.

Courtney Pazin can find a typo underneath a typewriter and is a formidable waterwoman.

Toby Petersen weathers small tweaks with a sharp tongue and quick mouse stroke.

Blair Harris, Ashley Huck and Walter Blair Tom are gracious and a fountain of local nuggets.

Steven Cox poured over early pages with tremendous love. In more ways than one.

Laura Arciniegas breaks through the dark clouds with extremely creative grammar suggestions.

My mother, Karen Sixt, gave me the treasured gifts of turnkey organization, never procrastinating and dry humor. Even though she wishes that I wouldn't write anything racier than *The Bridges of Madison County* (sorry Mom!), she never denies me access to her very hot dryer—The Inferno. I love you, Mom.

Thank you for your open doors and inspiration: AAA, Bolinas Border Patrol, Bolinas People's Store, Bruce Lee, Burt's Bees, Cafe Meuse, Chuck Palahniuk, Coast Cafe, Costco, Da Fin, Dr. Bronner's, Dunya Bistro, Fort Point Beer Company, Home Depot, Hunter S. Thompson, Instinct Clothing, Jell-O, Kit Kat, Kurt Vonnegut Jr., Lowe's, Lydia Millet, Matthew McConaughey, Netflix, Nickelodeon, Orangina, Patagonia, Peace of Mind, Ralph Waldo Emerson, Redbox, Smiley's Schooner Saloon, Staples, The Avenue Inn, *The Karate Kid*, *The Stormrider Guide North America*, Tinkers Burgers, Tom Hardy and Yeti Coolers.

About the Author

Thomas with City Surf Project, San Francisco. Photo by Olivia

VanDamme.

Made in the USA
San Bernardino, CA
12 March 2020